FLETCH, TOO

FLETCH, TOO

Gregory Mcdonald

WARNER BOOKS

A Warner Communications Company

The characters in Fletch, Too *are fictitious. Any resemblance to persons living or dead is coincidental.*

Warner Books, Inc., 666 Fifth Avenue, New York, NY 10103

A Warner Communications Company

Printed in the United States of America

First Printing: October 1986

10 9 8 7 6 5 4 3 2 1

Book design: H. Roberts

Library of Congress Cataloging-in-Publication Data

Mcdonald, Gregory, 1937–
    Fletch, too.

    I. Title.
PS3563.A278F513   1986   813'.54   85-41001
ISBN 0-446-51326-1

Dedicated to the wananchi.
Also dedicated to Joyce and Arthur Greene.
With special thanks to Kathy Eldon and Alexey Braguine.

What astounded Fletch was that the letter written to him was signed *Fletch*.

2

"Do you, Irwin Maurice Fletcher, promise to love, honor, serve, and support in all the ways a man can support a woman . . ." the Preacher shouted. Down the bluff the wind was whipping up whitecaps on the Pacific Ocean. A curtain of hard rain was visible a couple of miles offshore. ". . . cherish, respect, encourage, relinquish all interests and endeavors which do not serve the marriage, until death do you part?"

"Who wrote this?" Fletch asked.

At his side, wind whipping her skirt, Barbara said, "I did. You never gave me a chance to discuss it with you."

"Let's discuss it now."

Behind them on the bluff overlooking the sea stood their wedding guests, coat collars up, holding on to their hats.

"Be a good sport," Barbara said. "Say you do. We'll have plenty of time to discuss it."

"That's what I'm afraid of."

Barbara said to the Preacher, "He says, 'I do.' "

The Preacher looked at Fletch. "Do you do?"

"I guess I do."

"And do you, Barbara Ralston, promise to be a wife to this man, to the best of your abilities?"

"I do."

The Preacher then began to read interminably from some word-processor printout. Some rabbits built their hutch in a dell. Spring rains came, and the hutch got flooded out. They built a new hutch in a high place. The winds knocked it over . . .

Watching the storm approaching from the sea, Fletch suspected the wedding party was going to get flooded out and blown over, too.

The wedding had been planned for two o'clock Saturday afternoon. Fletch had gotten all his copy in by two o'clock, shaved in the men's room at the newspaper, and had reached his wedding at two-forty.

"Surprised to see you here," Fletch said to Frank Jaffe, the editor of the *News-Tribune.* "Thought you pretend employees don't exist Saturdays."

"I've been standing in for you at various police stations and courts the last three days," Frank said. "Thought I might have to stand in for you today at your wedding, too."

"You almost did." Two pickup trucks with their tail-gates down were parked across the field. In the bed of one truck, delicatessen food was laid out; in the bed of the other, plastic glasses, liquor, and ice. "Are all the various charges against me dropped? Can I get through an airport without being arrested?"

Frank tasted his drink. "Good follow-up on that law-yer's murder in this morning's edition. Got the big Sunday wrap-up in for tomorrow?"

"Yes, Frank."

"How about the big exposé of Ben Franklyn for tomor-row?"

"Ben Franklyn will be exposed in Sunday's newspaper, Frank. Pages and pages of it. With pictures."

"You've been working day and night since Monday."

"Very nearly."

"You look half asleep."

"Frank . . ."

"Have a nice honeymoon." Frank smiled. "You need the rest."

Alston Chambers said, "Fletch, thanks for coming. Being best man at a wedding without a groom was becoming a real strain."

"If you come across any hot stories on your honeymoon," Frank said, "be sure and phone them in. We may have found your talent in investigative reporting."

Alston looked down at Fletch's jeans and sneakers. "Didn't have time to change, uh?"

"Alston, I'm here, I shaved, I'm employed, I get to go on a honeymoon."

"I mean avalanches. Mud slides." Frank finished his drink. "Major earthquakes. Airplane crashes. Train wrecks."

Alston said, "I left some clothes for you at the City Desk. Didn't they tell you?"

"No."

Frank continued, "Mass murders. Acts of terrorism, like, you know, airport bombings."

Alston took Fletch by the elbow. "Your bride, having noticed you're here, would like you to go over and stand next to her in front of the Preacher. That's integral to the wedding."

"Be sure and phone in," Frank said. "If you get any good stuff."

Fletch said to his mother, "I'm surprised to see you here."

A long-stemmed flower bobbing from her hat hit Fletch in the eye as Josephine Fletcher leaned forward to kiss her son. "I wouldn't miss your first wedding for anything."

"This is the only wedding I have planned," Fletch said.
She waved airily. "After this, you're on your own."

" 'After this'?"

Josie scanned his clothes. "I guess you're dressed appropriately for a picnic next to the sea."

She was dressed in watered silk.

"I've been working."

"Barbara's mother was quite certain you wouldn't show up at all. She says you never do."

"Where is she? I've never met the lady."

"So she says. She's the one over there, in jodhpurs."

"Of course."

Josie scanned the bush. "I don't see where she parked her elephant."

"Elephant?"

Cindy took Fletch's other elbow. "The Preacher says, if you don't get over there, all hell will break loose."

Fletch turned and shook her hand. "Can't thank you enough, Cindy, for everything. You've helped Barbara get ready for our skiing honeymoon. You've helped me keep my job."

Cindy took the hand of a young woman standing next to her. "I feel this is as much our wedding as yours."

"It is." Fletch shook the hand of the other woman. "Have a nice life."

"Fletch," Alston said, looking harried, "this person says she has to meet you right now. Her name is Linda."

"I don't suppose this is a very good time to tell you this." Linda pulled his shirt out of his jeans. She cupped the palms of her hands against the skin of his waist. "I'm in love with you."

"You've never seen me before."

"I see you now. This is it, for me. Wildly, passionately in love." Her eyes said she was serious.

"Alston, how much are you paying this person?"

Alston sighed.

Fletch said to Linda, "I'm just about to get married."

"Really?" Sticking her chin out, she slid her hands up his sides.

"That's why we're all here," Fletch said. The wind was beginning to come up. "Standing around in this horrible place."

Alston said, "I think weddings make some people romantic."

Linda asked, "When are you returning from your honeymoon?"

"Two weeks. We're going skiing in Colorado."

"Don't break anything," she said.

"I'll try not to."

"Because I'm going to be your next wife."

"You are?"

"I've decided that." Linda looked like what she was saying was entirely reasonable. "In fact, you might as well skip this wedding with Barbara altogether."

"Boy," Alston said. "Getting you married is something I'll never try again."

"Was she serious?"

"Call me when you get back," Linda said. "I work with Barbara."

"Oh, nice." Fletch was being guided strongly by the elbow across the field. "Actually, she is beautiful."

"Barbara?" Alston asked.

Fletch said, "Linda."

"Oh, boy."

The wind had come up enough so Fletch had to speak loudly to the woman in jodhpurs. "Hello, Barbara's mother! How are you?"

The woman looked at him as if accosted. "Who are you?"

Fletch tucked in his shirt. "Don't worry. You're not gaining a son."

"Oh, my God."

"Nice to meet you, too."

In front of the Preacher, Fletch pinched Barbara's bottom. She wriggled. "Nice you could make the time."

"Hey, I filed two terrific stories this week." He shook hands with the Preacher.

To one side stood a man Fletch did not recognize. Standing alone, he was watching, not socializing. Middle-aged, he wore khaki trousers, khaki shirt, blue necktie, and a zippered leather jacket. His eyes were light blue. He held a sealed manila envelope.

Fletch said, "I just got a marriage proposal."

"Are you seriously considering it?" Barbara asked.

The bride wore walking shoes, leg warmers collapsed around her calves, skirt and sweater. She carried a bouquet of flowers.

Fletch said, "Nice posies."

"They're forget-me-nots. Alston remembered them."

Fletch looked across the field at the pickup trucks. "Someone arranged for caterers, too."

"Alston."

Fletch looked at Alston. "Guess I picked the right best man."

Alston shrugged. "Didn't have anything else to do. I'm an unemployed lawyer."

"And," Barbara said, "Alston has packed all your skiing things. And brought them to the airport. And checked them in."

Fletch looked at Cindy. "I'm getting chewed out here."

"Without Alston and Cindy. . ." Barbara's voice trailed off in the wind.

Alston touched the Preacher's arm as if searching for a starter button. "Sir?"

The Preacher smiled. "I've learned to wait until the bride and groom stop arguing. It makes for a nicer ceremony."

Alston said, "The weather . . ."

The Preacher looked out to sea. "Ominous."

The end of the allegory regarding rabbits was entirely blown away in the wind, despite the Preacher's shouting. Fletch wondered if he would ever know where the rabbits finally set up hutch.

The wind abated enough so that the Preacher could be heard to yell, "With the powers invested in me by the State of California, I now declare you man and wife. What God has put together, let no man put asunder."

A heavy raindrop fell on Fletch's nose.

Immediately Linda broke between the bride and groom and kissed the groom on the mouth.

"What about woman?" Fletch tried to say.

Cindy was kissing Barbara.

Hand on the back of his neck, Linda said, "Next time, baby. You and me."

The Preacher was kissing Barbara.

Alston shook Fletch's hand. "I do divorces."

"My vows seemed longer than her vows."

"I'm sure it always seems that way."

Barbara's mother was kissing Barbara.

The middle-aged man dressed in khaki came through the crowd. He handed Fletch the envelope.

"Thanks," Fletch said.

Immediately there were splotches of rain on the envelope.

Alston was kissing Barbara.

In the envelope were two passports, two thick airline ticket folders, a wad of bills, and a letter.

Fletch said, "Barbara?"

Frank Jaffe was kissing Barbara.

The man in khaki already was up on the road getting into a sports car. He had said nothing.

"Barbara . . ."

Dear Irwin:

What a moniker your mother hung on you. As soon as I heard that was who you were to be, Irwin

Maurice, I said to myself, There's nothing I can do for him. With a name like that, either he'll be a champ or a dolt.

Which is it?

I'm mildly curious.

After having missed out on your whole life, I didn't want to break a perfect record by attending your wedding.

How curious are you?

Enclosed is a wedding present, which you may take anyway you want. You may take the money, cash in the tickets, and buy your bride a nice set of china or something. That's probably what I would do. Or, if you're mildly curious about me, you and your bride can come visit me in my natural habitat. Squandering money is always fun, too.

Seeing you've now put yourself in the way of being a father yourself (at least you've gotten married), I thought we could meet agreeably.

If you do come to Nairobi, I've made a reservation for you and Barbara at the Norfolk Hotel.

Maybe I'll see you there.

Fletch

The rain was making the ink run on the page.

"Barbara!"

It was raining hard. Across the field, people were dashing for their cars. As Josephine walked, the flower blossom from her hat bobbed in front of her face. Men were throwing tarpaulins over the beds of the pickup trucks.

"What's that?" Alston asked.

Hundred-dollar bills were fluttering out of Fletch's hand and blowing in the wind. Alston scurried around picking them up.

On the road, Barbara was getting into a car with her mother.

"Where's Nairobi?" Fletch handed Alston the dripping letter.

"Nairobi? East Africa? Kenya?" Reading the letter, Alston tried to protect it from the wind and the rain with his body. "Fletch! Your father!"

On the road, cars were going off in each direction. Josephine Fletcher was nowhere in sight. Even the pickup trucks went in different directions.

"Fletch, this has to be from your father. You always said he was dead."

"He always was dead."

Together they looked at the faint lines under the running ink of the writing paper.

"What the hell," Alston said. "Your plane for Denver leaves at six o'clock."

Peering inside the envelope, Fletch said, "These tickets are for a plane to London, leaving at seven-thirty."

Only a few cars were left on the road.

"Alston, where is my mother staying?"

"At the Hanley Motor Court. On Caldwell, just off the freeway north."

"Do you suppose that's where she's gone?"

"Of course." Alston shivered. "We're soaking wet."

"Oh, yeah."

Fletch took the illegible letter from Alston and stuffed it back in the envelope. "If you see Barbara, tell her I'll meet her at the airport."

"Where are you going?"

Rain ran down the faces of the two young men as they looked at each other.

Jogging up the slope to his car, Fletch slipped and fell. He landed on the envelope in the mud.

"Your father died in childbirth."

"Whose?"

"Yours."

They stood inside the door of Josephine Fletcher's room at the Hanley Motor Court. She had changed into slacks, blouse, and open sweater. He was dripping wet.

He clutched the muddy envelope to his side.

"That's what you've always said."

"You need a hot shower."

"You've always said that, too."

"Mostly, for you, I've recommended cold showers." Josie turned on the light in the bathroom. "You're muddy, soaked, disheveled, and, my son, you look more exhausted than Hilary at the top of Mount Everest. What have you been doing to yourself?"

"Working. Getting married. Normal things."

"They don't seem to agree with you. But I will correct myself: for that particular wedding, you were indeed dressed appropriately. If I had known what was to happen, I would have worn a swimsuit."

"Your silk dress got watered."

Josie crossed the room to him. She put her hand out for the envelope under his arm. "Do you think you had some communication from your father? On your wedding day?"

"Yes. I think so." He put the muddy envelope on the bureau.

"That would be interesting," Josie said. "Exciting. To both of us. First, let me ask you: is your wedding over?"

"Not the marriage."

"That was it? So much milling about and shouting on a stormy bluff over the ocean?"

"We didn't have a backup plan."

"Only an hour ago you married a nice girl named Barbara," Josie said patiently. "You have, or you think you have, some communication from beyond the grave. However interesting and exciting it might be possibly to hear from your father, don't you think this is one of those particularly special times you really ought to be with your wife, no matter what?"

"She'll understand."

"Don't be too sure, sonny." Josie's face saddened. She turned toward the rain-streaked window. "Love and understanding have nothing to do with each other. I loved your father. I did not understand him. Why not? Was he too masculine, and I too feminine? Maybe the modern expectation that men and women really can understand each other is so false that it destroys marriages. As a woman, however, I will report to you that having a man present in a marriage means rather a lot to a woman." She turned to Fletcher again. "Like on your wedding day. And other notable occasions."

Fletch put his finger on the envelope. "This appears to be from my father. You've always given me this stupid line,

'Your father died in childbirth.' Never anything more, no matter how I've asked. I've always let you have the literary conceit of this stupid line. But the humor of it has worn as thin as my skin at the moment."

"You're curious?"

Fletch took a deep breath. "Mildly."

"What I'm saying, sonny, is that I see your possibly hearing from your father causes you to do exactly as he would have done."

"What's that?"

"Leave your bride alone on your wedding day."

"Did he do that to you?"

"He spent the entire wedding reception at the other end of the hangar removing, repairing and replacing the engine in the airplane we were about to use for our honeymoon."

"You were married in an airplane hangar?"

"By now you know how wind and rain on a bluff exposed to the sea can drown out the sweetest words a woman should ever hear. Consider how much of the wedding ceremony is heard in an airport aluminum hangar, with thirty seconds between scheduled takeoffs and landings."

Fletch smiled. "Are you sure you were married?"

"Are you sure you were married?"

"He wanted to be sure of the engine before he took his bride up in the plane."

"That was my kind thought, too, back when I expected to understand because I loved."

"What do you think now?"

"I think he was avoiding the reception, the congratulations, the handshakes, the slaps on the back, the jokes, and the reasonable questions obliging him to speak of our future with responsibility." Her eyes narrowed. "What are you doing?"

"My editor, Frank Jaffe, says I may have a talent for investigative reporting."

"This is your wedding day."

Fletch shrugged. "I've spent most of it working."

"Why is it considered the height of masculinity for a man to avoid the biggest emotional moments of his life by burying his head, and his body, in work?"

"Trickcyclists say a man's urge to work is as great as his sexual urge."

She smiled. "I haven't heard that slang for the mental health brigade in decades."

"I read that lately."

"Wouldn't you say work can also be man's way of avoiding emotional responsibility?"

"Okay. Super. You should know. But you're not going to evade my question now."

Josephine Fletcher colored. She said, "Your 'mild curiosity,' the mystery about your father, is not worth your taking two minutes from your wedding day."

Fletch shivered. "I don't know that for a fact."

"Get into the shower," his mother said. "Barbara won't want you sneezing all over her during your honeymoon. This traveler's court, or whatever it is, must have a washer-dryer for those Americans who choose to live all their lives entirely behind windshields. There are towels in the bathroom."

When he handed his clothes to her through the bathroom door, she said, "You know, I'm 'mildly curious,' too. Would you show me what you think you got from your father?"

Wrapped in a towel he crossed the room to the envelope. "Some tickets to Nairobi, Kenya, and some cash and a letter."

"Yes," she said. "If he's alive, he probably would be in Africa. I've thought that. May I see the letter?"

Between index finger and thumb, Fletch pulled the drenched, blued piece of paper out of the envelope and handed it to her.

Josie held it in two hands. As she looked at the washed-out, blank page, her face crinkled. "Oh, Irwin. Don't you see? There's nothing there."

"Ironic, and rather sad, that you are spending your wedding day with your mother."

Josie had ordered lunch for them from Room Service. They sat at odd angles obliged by the smallness of the motel room at the round table, taking the toothpicks out of their club sandwiches. Wind slashed rain against the window. "I say, more in worry than in bitterness, *See what your father has wrought?* First time you ever hear from him and you respond with behavior unnatural but typical of him."

"That much I've heard."

When Fletch bit into his sandwich a dollop of mayonnaise landed on the towel below his waist.

"Can't you at least telephone Barbara?"

"Not sure where she is."

"You just told me you're an investigative reporter. Surely you could find her."

"I've told Alston, my best man, to tell her I'd meet her at the airport."

"What does that mean?" Josie's bite of her sandwich was so small, mayonnaise had no chance to escape her.

"I want to do some thinking."

Her eyes widened. "You're not honestly thinking of going to Nairobi?"

He shrugged. "When will we ever get another chance?"

"Oh, Irwin! This man ignores you all your life; we presume him dead; and suddenly he snaps his fingers and you cancel your honeymoon and fly halfway around the world to meet him?"

"It could be a honeymoon. Barbara might like it."

Fletch remembered. Growing up, he had not been exactly the center of Josie Fletcher's universe either. There were her detective novels, always. He called them her *defective* novels. Because none had sold particularly well, there had had to be a lot of them. Other people made jokes about his mother's books. She had not written many novels, people said, she had written one novel many times. People joked that her publisher kept her writing one novel until she got it right. True, her producing murder and mayhem for quiet libraries throughout the land had kept them reasonably sheltered and reasonably fed. For that he was grateful to her.

Josie Fletcher lived in a world in which fictional characters had reality and real people were forgotten, blinked at, treated vaguely. The characters in her novels seldom had breakfast, lunch, and dinner all in the same day, never had cuts on their elbows, black eyes, broken fingers, itchy pubic hairs, or teachers deeply mistaken in their student's mathematical potential. They never went shopping to replace trousers that had risen up the shank of the leg or split in the back when the wearer stooped for a drink from the school water bubbler.

Independence was not something for which Fletch had ever had to strive. There had been moments when he had deeply resented it.

Yet here he was, on his wedding day, in a moldy motel room, having a sandwich with his mother, listening to her surprise at his expressing "mild curiosity" regarding his father. She had never, never told him about their marriage.

In fact, he was curious about both of them. Always had been.

"Why haven't you?" he asked.

"Why haven't I what?"

"Ever told me about my father, your marriage?"

"Fear and fairness."

"Fear?"

"Your masculinity, too, my son, is something I've never been able to come to grips with. Don't think a mother doesn't know. You've been ripping your jeans on garden fences since you were nine years old."

In front of his mother, Fletch blushed. "Men aren't born virgins, you know."

"You weren't, at any rate."

"A man has nothing to give up but his energy." Fletch laughed.

"Oh, God."

"I can't help it if I'm energetic."

"Is that what you call it?"

"May I have some of your french fries?"

"Of course. Do keep up your energy."

"I had pizza about three this morning. Supper or breakfast. I don't know which."

"Despite all my last chapters, not all mysteries have solutions. How does a mother explain to a son that she doesn't understand a husband, a father? That she was in a marital situation she doesn't understand?"

"By beginning with Chapter One?"

"And there's the element of fairness. I could have spewed forth what I thought about your father, my confusion, my hurt, my puzzlement, the *mystery*, but he wasn't around, you see, to defend himself, to give you his side of whatever story. I loved him, you see."

"You could have told me he left you, not that he *died*, for Christ's sake."

"I never knew that, you see." Her face turned whiter. "You show up today with, frankly, a blank piece of paper . . ."

Fletch watched his mother try to gather together in one hand another quarter of her three-decker sandwich.

"You know that we had to have your father declared assumed dead, after seven years. Otherwise, I couldn't have married Charles."

"I remember him."

"He wasn't with us long, was he? Or Thad."

"You've kept the name Fletcher."

"Well, I had published books under that name, you see, and it was your name. And Charles, and Thad, and . . . weren't your father." She wiped under her eyes with her paper napkin. "It was the *impossibleness* of your father that I loved. If that blank piece of paper you showed me means anything, if he did go somewhere, I would have loved to have gone with him."

"But you say you didn't understand him."

"Oh, who the hell understands anybody? Damn fools keep asking me why I write mystery stories. Maybe because there's a big mystery in my life I've never been able to solve. So, neurotically, I keep setting up simulated mysteries and arriving at simulated solutions. Frustrated practicing."

"Writers have an uncontrollable compulsion to control compulsion," Fletch said. "I read that somewhere, too. Remembered it, in my effort to understand you."

"Lots of luck," she said.

"Chapter One." Fletch snuck a look at her wristwatch. "I'm trying to make a decision here. Am I flying to Denver, Colorado, or Nairobi, Kenya?"

"I don't know what to tell you."

"Chapter One," he repeated.

"Chapter One," she said. "High School. Montana. I was the pretty little thing. Cheerleader. Honor student."

"I've read this book," Fletch said. "Several times. And he was the big man on campus, president of the class, captain of the football team."

"Far from it. He was way out."

"Sorry. Wrong novel."

"Way out, skidding his overpowered motorcycle around his parents' dirt-poor ranch. Bright enough. He once wrote this paper for English class, this long, somber, brilliant analysis of a Shakespearean sonnet. The teacher gave him an A-plus-plus, and complimented Walter in class. Walter roared with laughter. He told everybody he had written the 'Shakespearean' sonnet himself and then analyzed it. Nearly destroyed the teacher."

"Ah," said Fletch. "So it was Daddy who wrote Shakespeare."

"When they expelled him for that—"

"They expelled him for that?"

"Suspended him. At the time, the object of education was obedience, not intellectual freedom. Has anything changed? Anyway, Walter took an airplane without permission from a neighboring ranch—"

"He could fly a plane in high school?"

"No one knew he could. First he buzzed the high school a few times, while it was in session. Then he bombed it. With a volume called *The Collected Plays of Shakespeare*. Made a perfect hit, too. Smashed the skylight over the stairwell. The book and all this glass came crashing down three floors."

"And you've never wanted to tell me about this man?"

"Wild. You mentioned football. One Saturday at a home game, suddenly he appeared on the field, standing up in the saddle of his motorcycle. He caught a pass, sat down, roared down the field and through the goalposts, ball cradled under one arm."

"Did he ever spend any time in jail?"

"Some. He was so handsome, so . . ." Josie shrugged. ". . . energetic, everyone should have loved him. Everyone hated him. Everything he did jeered at everything we held sacred. He jeered at the school by fooling the teacher with *his* Shakespearean sonnet. He jeered at football by saying, If the object is to get the football down the field, through the goalposts, use a motorcycle. He'd show up at school dances drunk, and dance energetically, *satirically*, I now realize. Everybody else would go home."

"Dance with you?"

"To my embarrassment, yes."

"What was a nice girl like you doing with a rogue like him?"

"Maybe I had a little understanding of him. At least between someone very feminine and someone very masculine, if not much ability to understand, there is a very strong chemistry? Electricity?"

"Sex?"

"He wasn't an outlaw. As soon as everybody in the town thought he was, and the real baddies began to talk as if he were one of their own, Walter dressed in as close an approximation of a suit and tie as he and his family possessed, and went down to the local baddy hangout, a really horrible roadhouse about eight miles out of town, and started a riot I expect they're still talking about. He jeered at *everybody*."

"How old was he then?"

"Would you believe fifteen?"

"How could you not tell me about him?"

"Energetic," his mother said. "Bright, handsome, and energetic. Saw things his own way, and never asked for agreement. I mean, it's not everybody who is expelled from school *and* the local roadhouse. I thought him simply marvelous."

"Is that why you've never sought agreement from me?"

Josie looked at her son from under lowered lids. "Anyway, we were married literally over my father's dead body. I've told you your grandfather died of a heart attack during my senior year of high school."

"Yes. Must put that fact in my medical folder, if I live long enough."

"Walter had a flying job. Flying ranchers around, mining executives, emergency medical equipment, out-of-state crop-dusting, in season. Sometimes, frankly, I wasn't absolutely sure where he was. Weather's always a problem in a job like that." Josie poured coffee for them both. "I got pregnant immediately. I thought that was the right thing to do, that was the way life was, that we both wanted it. It never occurred to me you were supposed to *think* about such things. We were buying a house trailer. I thought we were perfectly happy."

"What do you guess he thought?"

Josie sighed. "Everyone was telling this *boy*, Walter, that he was married and about to be a father and ought to give up flying and riding motorcycles. That he ought to give up being *Walter*. At the time, I thought such talk was natural, too. I've wondered since how he heard it."

"Come on, get to the good part: me."

"You were born ten days ahead of expectations. Walter had promised he would be with me when you were born. In fact, he was across the state. My mother telephoned him the good news. He said he would take off and fly home right away. There being a major storm in his path, he was advised against flying. He took off. He never arrived."

"He crashed?"

"Seven years later we were able to assume him dead. After the snows melted in the spring, a search was made for his plane. It was never found."

"He died in childbirth."

"An enigmatic statement, for which I apologize. I always thought it rather graceful. What I mean by it is, What was in his mind when he climbed into that airplane, when he took off, while he flew alone across the state of Montana in the dark, presumptively to his wife and son, me and you? Do you understand? What was in his mind at that point has always been more important to me, in a way, than whether he lived or died."

"Maybe I understand. A little."

"Who *was* Walter? Who *is* he?"

"I need my clothes."

Josie looked at him as if awaking suddenly. "Where are you going?"

"I don't know."

"When will you know?"

Fletch said, "It's a long drive to the airport."

"May I kiss the bride, too?"

Fletch decided where he wanted to go only as he walked down the airport corridor with the muddy envelope under his arm and saw Barbara and Alston waiting outside the gate.

"Where have you been?" Barbara asked.

"Where did you go?" Fletch asked.

"Where did you go?"

"I didn't know where you went."

Alston rolled up his eyes.

"Have Cindy and her friend gone?" Fletch asked.

Barbara said, "They've gone."

"Where's our luggage?" Fletch asked.

Barbara said, "It's gone."

"I checked it in this morning," Alston said. "So you wouldn't have to be bothered with it at this point."

"It's gone?"

"It's gone."

"We need to get it back."

"Oh, no," Alston said. "It's gone."

"The plane's about to go," Barbara said.

"It hasn't gone," Fletch said.

Alston looked at his watch.

"We're not going?" Barbara asked.

"We're going." Fletch said to Alston, "You didn't tell her?"

"I'm not going to."

"We're not going to Colorado."

"Our luggage is," Barbara said.

"Must get it back," Fletch said.

Alston hit his forehead with the palm of his hand. "Skis."

"Come on," Fletch said. "Let's go."

They were rushing up the corridor.

"We're not going?" Barbara asked.

"I've got the tickets," Alston said. "Turn them in. I've got the baggage tickets. Get the luggage."

Barbara said, "We're not going."

"We are going," said Fletch. "Alston, we need to get the luggage to British Air at the International Terminal."

"The plane's changed?" Barbara asked.

"We're changing planes."

"For Colorado?"

"London."

"London, Colorado?"

"Kenya."

"London, Kenya?"

"Nairobi, Kenya."

"Nairobi, Kenya!"

"Africa."

"Africa!"

"East Africa."

Barbara mouthed the words: "East Africa . . ."

"Didn't you say you'd follow me to the ends of the earth?"

"Never! You can't even find a pizza parlor in Malibu!"

In the terminal's main concourse, Barbara jumped ahead of Fletch, turned around, and stopped. Facing Fletch, she put her fists on her hips.

"Fletch! What's going on?"

"London," Fletch said. "Then we're going on to Kenya."

Alston had kept walking.

"Tell me what's happening!"

"We've got a wedding present," Fletch said. "A trip to Nairobi, Kenya."

"Who from? Tell me another." Barbara's face flushed. "Fletch! You accepted an assignment from the newspaper on our honeymoon!"

"No, no. Nothing like that."

Flapping boarding passes, airline tickets, baggage stubs, Alston was at the airline's courtesy information booth clearly straining the attendant's courtesy.

"You did too!"

"Would I do that to you?"

"I'll be damned if I'm going to sit in some hotel room, or some, some grass shack while you run miles in circles trying to fill up one damned inch of that damned newspaper! Not on my honeymoon!"

"I told you: the trip is a present. A wedding present. It will be fun."

"I'll bet. A present from the newspaper!"

"No. Not from the newspaper."

"Who else would give you a trip to Africa?"

The courteous man at the information counter now had a phone to each ear while also, apparently, listening to Alston.

"My father."

Barbara's eyes popped. "Your father?"

"I guess."

"You didn't say, *I do* at the wedding, you said, *I guess I do*. Now you're saying you *guess* you got a wedding present of a trip to Africa from father?"

"It's turned into a highly conjectural day."

At the counter, Alston's lips were moving rapidly.

"You've never had a father. Or you've had four of them, or something."

"What's the difference?"

"What father?"

"The one who died."

"You've inherited something?"

"No. We really don't have time to discuss this now, Barbara."

"You didn't have time to discuss the wedding, either."

"And it happened, see? It came off with a hitch. All right. Things work out."

Barbara wagged her head. "This can't work out."

"Sure it can."

"I can't go to Kenya."

"We haven't had any shots, have we?"

"I don't have a passport!"

"Oh, that." Fletch reached into the muddy envelope. "You have a passport." He handed it to her.

Alston was striding toward them, smiling.

"Alston," Fletch said, "we haven't had any shots."

"You only need them for medical reasons," Alston said. "Not legal reasons."

"I'm glad you became a lawyer."

"Yeah." Alston glanced at Barbara. "Don't forget: I do divorces."

"Where did this picture of me come from?" Barbara said into her passport.

Fletch glanced at it over her shoulder. "It's a nice one."

"Okay." Alston was sorting various tickets and stubs in his hands. "Your tickets to Colorado are canceled. Not sure I'll be able to get your money back."

"Can we get the luggage back?"

"That's my green sweater," Barbara said at her passport picture.

"What they're going to try to do is get your luggage off that plane, then they'll send it over to the International Terminal, British Air, and get it aboard your flight to London, checked straight through to Nairobi."

Fletch put Barbara's passport back in the muddy envelope. "We won't know if our luggage is with us until we get to Nairobi."

"The skis," Barbara said.

"Can't separate the luggage now." Alston shook his head. "No way. Things are too confusing as it is."

"Are you confused?" Barbara asked. "I'm not confused."

Alston glanced at his watch. "We've got to get over to the International Terminal quick-quick. Got to tell them what your connecting flight to Nairobi is."

"Quick-quick." Fletch grabbed Barbara's elbow.

"We're not going skiing," Barbara said. "We packed ski clothes! Nothing but ski clothes!"

"Barbara, we have to hurry."

"Where?"

"International Terminal," Fletch said.

"British Air," Alston said.

They were dashing across the concourse.

"London, England," Fletch said.

"Passport Control," Alston said.

"Nairobi, Kenya," Fletch said.

"Fletch! I told my mother I'd call her from Colorado!"

"Can't stop," Fletch said.

"Tonight!"

Fletch steered her into the revolving door.

"Ain't married life fun?" After he went through the revolving door himself, he said, "So far?"

"All my mother wanted to do was meet you." Barbara fastened her seat belt.

"I met her. At the wedding."

"Would you believe she really wanted to meet you *before* the wedding?"

"I met her before the wedding. She was wearing jodhpurs. Right? She seemed real surprised to see me."

"Dismayed, more likely. She arranged dinner for us every night last week. You never made it. Not once."

"I was working. Did I tell you I have a job?"

"And you're dragging me halfway around the world to meet your father?"

"Maybe."

"What do you mean, 'maybe'?"

"He's known to evade important occasions." Buckled up, Fletch put the side of his face against the back of his seat.

"You're going to sleep, aren't you?"

"Barbara, I have to. I haven't slept in days and nights, and days, and . . ."

Barbara sighed. "How long before we get to Nairobi, Kenya?"

"Two days."

"Two days!"

"Two nights? Maybe three days."

"Fletch. Wake up. Get your head off my shoulder. Listen to what the steward's saying about what to do when the airplane crashes."

"That's okay," Fletch mumbled. "You're coming with me."

"Oh, my God! Seven-twenty on our wedding night, and he's asleep!"

++++++++++++++

"The thing is," Fletch said, "I never knew there was a possibility my father is alive."

Many, many hours later on the flight from London to Nairobi, they were terribly scrunched up. The airplane was full. The seats were narrow and close to each other. There was hand luggage spilling out from under every seat.

"Did your mother know? Did she know there was a possibility he was alive?"

"I think she convinced herself he was dead. To keep her pride. To keep her sanity. In order to marry again, she had to legally assume him dead after seven years."

"I guess in order to go to court to declare your husband dead, you have to believe he's dead."

"But she never really knew. When I'd ask questions about him, you know, growing up, her answers would always be so glib, so casual, you know? I'd get the idea the topic wasn't worth discussing."

"Maybe it wasn't."

"She says she loved him, though."

"What sort of things would she tell you?"

"She'd say, 'Hey, I was only married to your father ten months, and I never understood him.' "

"Then what would she say?"

" 'How do you spell "license"?' "

"Why would she say that?"

"Well, you know, she writes these detective novels. And she never could spell. She'd ask me to look words up in the dictionary for her. It was her way of getting rid of me."

"What did you know about your father?"

"I knew he was a pilot. I knew, or thought I knew, he died about when I was born. Therefore, I always assumed he died in a plane crash shortly after I was born. Or before. I knew my mother was alone when she gave birth to me. I didn't realize she was awaiting a husband who never showed up. A child accepts what he's told."

"Did you ever see a picture of your father?"

Fletch scanned his memory. "Never. That's odd, isn't it? Naturally, there would be pictures of your father around, if he were dead."

"But not if there was a possibility he was alive, and had abandoned you both."

"So that possibility must have been very much in my mother's mind."

"Very much, I'd say."

The areas under the seats in front of them were filled,too.

Instead of waiting at Heathrow eight hours for their connecting flight to Nairobi or finding a place to sleep, Barbara and Fletch had bussed into London. Fletch had no clothes but the jeans and shirt he was wearing. Barbara insisted upon buying sweaters. They had lunch in a not-very-good place. They bought books. They got lost. They had to taxi back to the airport.

"This little guy just came up to me after the wedding, while everyone but the groom was kissing the bride, and just handed me this envelope."

"I didn't see him."

"He was there, I swear it. He didn't say a word. Just handed me the envelope and left."

Barbara asked, "Are you sure he wasn't your father?"

"I would think if he were, my mother would have recognized him."

"It's been a long time."

"Still . . . they knew each other all through school."

"Maybe your mother didn't even see him. We were outdoors, somewhat of a crowd, bad weather . . ."

"And you never know whether my mother is seeing real people or socializing with figments of her imagination."

"Right," Barbara said. "She must have been deeply hurt by all this."

"And deeply puzzled."

Barbara smiled. "The mystery Josie Fletcher couldn't solve. Better not let her fans in the libraries know."

"Her only fans are in the libraries, and are silent."

"What else was in the envelope?"

"The tickets, the passports, ten one-hundred-dollar bills, and the letter."

"You haven't shown me the letter."

"There's nothing to see." Fletch reached under the seat in front of him and picked up the envelope. "It all washed away in the rain."

He handed her the wrinkled piece of paper.

"That's sad." She stared at it in her hand. "Maybe your mother could have recognized the handwriting. How do you know it was from your father?"

"It was signed 'Fletch.' "

"What's his real name?"

"Walter."

"Walter. I wonder how I would have thought of you as a Walter junior."

"A fletcher by any other name is still an arrow maker."

"So what did the letter say?" She handed it back to him.

"In fact, it said something about my name." He leaned forward as much as he could to put the envelope back. "Something about not liking my names, Irwin Maurice, something about my mother's giving me these names, not him, or not with his agreement, as if he'd had nothing to do with it."

"What are you talking about?"

He sat back again. "The letter read almost as if my mother gave the baby, me, these names which he didn't like, didn't relate to, on her own, and this made the baby, me, more her baby than his: that he couldn't relate to anyone named Irwin Maurice."

"Neither can you."

"But I've stuck around. I haven't disappeared."

"You disappear all the time."

"He said he was 'mildly curious' in meeting me and asked if I was 'mildly curious' in meeting him."

"That's the word he used? 'Mildly'?"

"Yes. 'Mildly.' But the airline tickets to Nairobi and back are expensive."

"Maybe he's rich."

"Maybe he was giving us each an out. He wrote I certainly didn't have to come if I didn't want. He said I could cash the tickets in and buy you a set of china or something."

"A set of china," Barbara said. "I might have liked that."

"You'll never see your china, but you will see Kenya."

"Maybe this isn't from your father at all." Barbara wriggled uncomfortably in her seat. "Maybe somebody was trying to get you out of the country for a while. One of these stories you've been investigating."

"I suppose that's possible."

"Keep you out of court, keep you from raising more trouble, or something."

"Maybe everyone on the newspaper took up a collection

to get rid of me. Maybe the return tickets are no good." Fletch smiled.

"Maybe a wild-goose chase."

Fletch asked, "Aren't you 'mildly curious'?"

"Only mildly."

Fletch continued looking at Barbara.

"I'm trying to say something here," she said.

"I know. What?"

"I don't think it's good for you to be more than 'mildly curious.' You know what I mean?"

"So I won't be more than mildly disappointed?"

"Yeah," Barbara said. "Something like that."

"*Jambo*," the customs official in Nairobi airport said. He eyed the two pairs of covered skis Fletch held upright.

Very carefully, Fletch said, "*Jambo.*"

"*Harbari?*" He was a short, pudgy, balding man in well-pressed shirt and trousers.

Fletch said, "*Habari.*"

"So you have been to Kenya before."

"Never," Fletch said. "Never been in Africa before."

"That's the way it is." The man chuckled softly. "Everyone in the world speaks Swahili."

Barbara said, "I've got to take off this sweater."

The two pairs of skis in their soft plastic covers had drawn the particular attention of the customs official to Barbara and Fletch. In fact, the two pairs of wrapped skis were drawing the attention of many people in Nairobi airport. These people stood in a loose circle around Fletch, Barbara, and the skis. Two of these people were in uniforms.

Nightsticks and handguns dangled from their belts. One carried a machine gun.

The customs official took his eyes off the wrapped skis long enough to look at the passports Fletch handed him. "Are you visiting Kenya for business or pleasure?"

"Pleasure," Barbara answered. "We were just married. Days ago. A million years ago."

Fletch then heard, for the first time, the sound he was to hear many times in Kenya, the little song exhaled on three notes: "Oh, I see."

The customs official made a note on his clipboard. "And what sort of shooting equipment is that, in the rifle covers, you are bringing into Kenya? Very long rifles, I think." He pointed the back of his pen at them as if they really needed pointing out.

"Oh, these." Fletch looked up and down the skis he held beside him. "These are for shooting down mountains."

The official looked alarmed. "Shooting down mountains? Is that possible?"

"Skis."

"Skis . . . Mombasa?"

Very carefully, Fletch said: "Mombasa."

"I have skied off Mombasa. Behind a speedboat." The official took the position of one skiing behind a speedboat, knees bent, hands forward to hold a towline. "The skis I used were short. Perhaps in proportion to the feet?" He looked down at Barbara's and Fletch's feet. "I don't think so."

"Snow skis."

"Oh, I see. I have seen those in films. This large, are they? You are in Kenya en route to someplace else."

Fletch was hoping that soon he could get to a men's room. "Not really."

"Where do you go after Kenya?"

"Home. Back to the States."

"You return to the United States? With the skis?"

Fletch craned his neck to look through the door of the controlled area to see if possibly anyone was waiting, looking for them. "Yes."

The official thought a long moment. "You always travel with snow skis, even to the equator?"

"No."

"There was some confusion," Barbara said.

"Oh, I see."

"At the airport. We ended up bringing the skis with us."

"At the airport, did you not know you were coming to Africa? Did you get on the wrong plane?"

"We knew," Fletch said. "We got on the right plane."

"So you knew what you were doing when you brought your snow skis to Kenya, just to bring them home again?"

"Well, that's the fact." Barbara looked at Fletch. "We did bring our skis to Africa."

"There is snow on Mount Kenya," the official conceded, "but it's at the top, you see. There are no skiing safaris. Perhaps you brought these snow skis to Africa to sell them. They are a curiosity."

"We can't sell them," Barbara said. "They're borrowed."

"Oh, I see. You borrowed skis to bring to Africa and home again."

"Fletch," Barbara said, "quite reasonably, this gentleman wants to know why we brought snow skis to equatorial Africa."

"Wait till I take off my sweater." Fletch leaned the skis against Barbara and wriggled out of his London-bought sweater. "Hot."

"Perhaps someone here could use snow skis for a wall decoration," mused the official. "Someone who has a very large wall."

"Originally we were going to Colorado," Fletch said. "Skiing."

"And you failed to get off the plane when it stopped in Colorado?"

"It didn't stop in Colorado," Barbara said. "If it had, I would have called my mother."

The official smiled at her.

Fletch said, "It's a little difficult explaining just why we have landed in Kenya carrying snow skis. I admit that."

The official wagged his head. "I love my job."

"We'll definitely take the skis with us when we leave," Fletch said.

"We have to return them," Barbara said. "They're borrowed."

"I would love to see them," the official said, "while they're here."

"Of course." Fletch opened the zipper on one of the ski covers. The man carrying the machine gun stepped back a pace. "There," Fletch said. "Skis."

The official seemed surprised. "And those . . ." He bent his knees again and now used his hands as paddles. ". . . those are ski walking sticks?"

"Ski poles."

The official concerned himself with his clipboard. "Snow skis are very large items to carry with you when you can't use them."

"Cumbersome, too," Barbara said.

Fletch said, "I'm very fond of them." He zippered the cover closed again.

"May I see what is in your luggage, please?" the official asked.

"Of course." Fletch handed the skis to Barbara and unzipped his large knapsnack. As he folded back the cover he saw on top of the clothes a book entitled *How to Screw Around*. "Oh, my," he said. He remembered Alston had packed for him. Quickly, he picked up the book and held it by his side.

The official stroked the palm of his hand over the nylon surface of Fletch's ski pants. "That feels beautiful," he said. "Like the skin of a woman. Do you wear these?"

Fletch swallowed. "When I go skiing."

"Oh, I see. These are skiing trousers."

"Yes."

The official's hand went layer through layer down the bag. "They're like moon clothes."

"We're not from the moon," Barbara said.

"They're ski clothes," Fletch said.

The official said, "This bag is full of ski clothes."

Fletch said, "I suppose it is."

"Usually when people come to Kenya for pleasure," the official said, "they bring shorts. Safari jackets. Sun hats. Swimsuits. Hiking boots."

Fletch said, "Oh, I see."

The official waved his hand at the bag, indicating it could now be closed. "I'm afraid you won't have a very good time in Kenya, if you insist on going snow-skiing."

Fletch dropped *How to Screw Around* back into the knapsack. "We'll try our best."

8

Fletch handed Barbara a one-hundred-dollar bill. "Would you please go to the exchange booth and get some local currency?"

Immediately when they came out of the controlled area five small boys had grabbed the skis and carried them on their shoulders out to the sidewalk. A man had grabbed the rest of the luggage. Others had just shouted *Taxi!* at them.

"Where are you going?"

"Men's room. We need taxi fare."

"What's the exchange rate?"

"Tit for tat. Roughly."

"Thanks."

There was only one other man in the men's room. Slim, he wore a full-length safari suit. Thinning hair was stretched across his pate. He had a pencil-thin moustache. He was washing at a basin.

Sitting in the cabinet, Fletch watched the man's brown

boots make the little movements on the floor a person makes while thinking he is standing still. The water was splashing into the basin.

The main door to the men's room opened. Heavy black shoes beneath dark trousers came into view beneath the cabinet door. The brown boots turned. The two men spoke a language Fletch didn't understand. He could barely hear it over the sound of the running water. Then one man shouted. The other man shouted. They both were shouting. The feet began moving, agitated. Forward, back, sideways, some sort of crazy dance. The brown boots became nearer the men's room door. One of the black shoes landed on the floor on its side, on the man's ankle. The black shoes pulled backward to the right. The brown boots turned and sprinted for the door. The water was still running.

Fletch came out of the cabinet, pulling up his jeans. He pressed the flat of his hand against his stomach. His other hand covered his mouth.

Blood was on the mirror, the white washbasins, the floor.

A man's body was in the corner, his neck twisted against the wall. His white shirt was soaked with blood, from just below the chest down. Some blood was on his dark trousers, as far down as his knees. His jaw was slack. His eyes, glassy as a stuffed animal's, stared toward the men's room door. On the side of the sink above his head was his bloody, streaked hand print.

Water was still running in the basin. A knife had been dropped into it. Water swirling around the knife was still bloody.

Fletch's two hands could not stop what was about to happen. He went to a basin nearer the door. He vomited. He rinsed out the basin. He vomited again.

After rinsing the sink a second time he stood against the basin a moment to steady himself. Then he rubbed cold water on his face, the back of his neck.

Using the bottom of his shirt around his hand, he opened the men's room door.

Eyes stinging, temples throbbing, knees shaking, Fletch tried to walk straight across the airport terminal while he tucked in his shirt.

The sunlight on the sidewalk outside the Nairobi airport was brilliant. Barbara was showing the taxi driver how to weight down one end of the skis with a knapsack so they could stick out of the trunk without falling. Many people stood around very interested in this problem of transporting skis by taxi.

Trembling, Fletch crossed the sidewalk directly to the taxi. He sat on the backseat. He rolled down the window. He sucked warm, dry air into his lungs.

Bending, Barbara looked through the back door of the taxi at him. "Fare to the Norfolk Hotel should be about one hundred and seventy shillings. I exchanged a hundred-dollar bill for local currency, inside, at the bank window." Adjusting to the light inside the taxi, her eyes narrowed. "What's the matter with you? What happened?"

"Get in, please."

She sat on the backseat. "Can't take a little jet lag?"

"Close the door, please."

"Do I look as badly as you do? Fletch, what's the matter?"

Speaking softly, he said, "I just saw someone get murdered. Stabbed to death. Blood." He tried to rub the brilliant sunlight out of his eyes. "Blood everywhere."

"My God! You're serious!" She sat closer to him on the seat. "Everywhere where?"

"Men's room."

She, too, spoke softly. "What do you mean, you *saw* a murder? My God, this is terrible."

At the back of the car, the driver was trying to arrange the trunk lid so it would not fly up and bounce as they went along the road.

Eyes closed, facedown, Fletch pressed his fingers against his forehead and cheekbones. "When I went into the men's room, a guy was standing at the basin washing his hands. I went into a cabinet. While I was sitting there, another guy came in. They began shouting at each other. Below the cabinet door I saw their feet get excited, do this crazy dance. There was a loud shout from one of them, agony, distress." Barbara put her arm over Fletch's shoulder. "I came out as quickly as I could. The second man, the man I hadn't seen before, was slumped in a corner, dead. There was blood everywhere, coming from just below his ribs. There was a bloody hand streak on the wall. His eyes were open, staring at the door. The water was still running in the basin. In the basin was a knife. The water in the basin was red."

"You're sure he was dead?"

"He wasn't blinking."

"My God, Fletch. What are we going to do?" She looked through her closed window to the airport terminal.

"I don't know. What can we do?"

"What have you done so far?"

"I've thrown up."

"You look it."

"Into one of the other basins. I cleaned up after myself."

"Nice boy." She took one of his hands in hers. "Do you think anyone else knows about this yet?"

Fletch looked through the window at the people standing on the sidewalk. "No one seems very excited."

"We must tell someone." Her hand went for the door handle.

"Wait a minute." He took her hand. "Let's think a minute."

"What good is thinking going to do? Something terrible has happened. Somebody got murdered. You saw it. We have to tell someone."

"Barbara, just wait a minute."

"Can you identify the murderer? The first man in the men's room?"

"Yes."

"What did he look like?"

"Middle-aged. Slim. Thinning, sandy hair. Pencil moustache. Khaki clothes. Safari jacket."

"What were they arguing about?"

"I couldn't tell. Foreign language. Portuguese, I think."

"Fletch, we have to tell someone."

"Barbara, you're not thinking."

"What's to think about? You saw a murder."

"We've just arrived in Kenya. We don't know how things are here. Because of the skis, the ski clothes, we made clowns of ourselves coming through customs."

"Come on. That was funny."

"Yeah. And the press will report we were not acting normally going through customs. We seemed confused."

"I am confused."

"I know. I've written reports like that. Barbara, we attracted the attention of the two gun-carrying soldiers."

"True."

"What are we doing in Kenya?"

"What are we doing in Kenya with skis?"

"We're here to meet my father. *Prove it.* There's this washed-out letter inviting us. *It's illegible!* We're not on very solid ground here."

"You're just reporting a murder."

"I don't want to have anything to do with a murder. This isn't California. We've just arrived in a foreign country. We don't know what it's like here. I go into a men's room. There's someone in there alive. I come out and report there is someone else in the men's room who is dead? And you expect people to believe I had nothing to do with it? Come on, Barbara. What would you think? I didn't come halfway around the world to be taken off immediately in handcuffs and leg irons to the local police warehouse."

"Did anyone notice you go into the men's room?"

"How do I know?"

"Or come out?"

"Barbara . . ."

"You're right. Until a better suspect comes along, you're the best the police would have."

"Just an airport incident."

"You have no evidence that there was another guy, a third guy, in the men's room?"

"Nothing but my word. And that's the word of a guy who has just arrived on the equator carrying skis and ski clothes, waving an illegible invitation from a man whom the courts in California declared dead years ago."

"Shaky ground."

"Without a leg to stand on."

"Fletch, we have been moving pretty fast here."

"Yeah. Lots of fun. Until something goes wrong."

Annoyed, Barbara looked through the window at the terminal again. "Why didn't your father meet us at the airport? He's a pilot. He has to know where the airport is!"

Fletch didn't say anything. He exhaled slowly.

"Your breath smells like an old cat's," Barbara said. "Do you still feel sick?"

"Good thing British Air didn't give us much breakfast."

The driver passed by Fletch's window.

"Barbara, don't say anything about this the driver can hear."

Barbara sighed. "Your decision."

++++++++++++++

Before starting the engine, the driver turned around in the front seat and looked at Fletch. *"Jambo."*

"Habari," Fletch breathed.

The driver's forehead wrinkled. *"Mzuri sana."*

"My husband's sick," Barbara said. "Must be something he ate."

For the first time, Fletch heard the two-note song, B flat, F: "Sorry."

In a land where people, even a broad-shouldered taxi driver, sang so sweetly, so gently, their simple courtesies, *"Oh, I see. Sorry,"* how could Fletch possibly have seen what he just saw? A clean, public lavatory turned into a blood-splattered, blood-streaked, blood-puddled room of horror in less time than it took for him to relieve himself. Like seeing a snake come out of a hen's egg. Again, Fletch rubbed his eyes with his fists. The man sat in a pool of blood, spraddle-legged on the floor in the corner of the room, his neck twisted, his eyes staring unblinking at the door, blood everywhere below his rib cage.

"Damn!" Barbara expostulated. "Your father didn't come to meet us at the airport."

Softly, Fletch said, "I guess he didn't."

As the taxi pulled away from the curb it passed a group of people packing into a van. From behind the van walked quickly the first man Fletch had seen in the men's room, thinning combed hair, pencil moustache: the murderer. He carried his safari jacket rolled up in his hand. Small sections of his khaki trousers were dark brown, wet.

Fletch said, "Hey, wait a minute."

The taxi slowed. The driver looked at Fletch through the rearview mirror.

Barbara asked, "Are you going to be sick?"

The man, the murderer, had his hand on the door handle of a parked car. He was looking around.

Fletch did feel sick again.

"Go ahead," Barbara said to the driver. "He'll be all right."

The taxi proceeded through the gate. The moment had passed.

Barbara took Fletch's hand onto her lap. "You going to be all right?"

"I'll be all right. Just a shock. The last thing I expected to see."

"It was the last thing someone did see." She squeezed his hand. "Welcome to Africa."

"What in hell are we doing here?"

"When you arrive at a ski lodge in Colorado you're handed a cup of hot chocolate."

"Somehow," Fletch said, "I don't think this welcoming was arranged by the Kenyan Tourist Bureau."

"No," Barbara said. "But I would have expected your father to be here. He arranged the tickets. He knew when we were arriving. Altogether, it would have been a help having him here."

Again, Fletch exhaled, heavily.

✦✦✦✦✦✦✦✦✦✦✦✦✦✦

Slowly, on the drive into Nairobi from the airport Fletch became more alert to his surroundings.

The taxi went at a sedate pace. Worriedly, the driver kept glancing in the rearview mirror. As they went along, the trunk lid bounced higher and higher.

The snow skis sticking out of the trunk of a taxi driving into Nairobi, Kenya, attracted a lot of attention. Other drivers smiled at them, blew their horns, waved at what appeared to be a joke or, at least, something funny. People on the sidewalks pointed. A few people seemed to know, or were able to figure out, what they were. Others just found two blue fangs sticking out the back of a flapping Mercedes funny enough.

As they began to go around a rotary, Fletch saw, on his left, a children's playground. Everywhere in the playground were oversize traffic signs, STOP, RAILROAD CROSSING, WAIT, WALK, CAUTION.

Fletch said, "People here like their kids."

Barbara frowned at him. "People everywhere like their kids."

"I've never seen an urban park dedicated to teaching kids traffic signs before."

The car slowed before making a U-turn to pull up at the front door of the Norfolk Hotel.

"Oh, no," Barbara said.

"Oh, no, what? It's beautiful."

The hotel looked like a Tudor hunting lodge in tropical sunlight. In front, a deep, covered veranda, a bar/restaurant, ran half the length of the building.

"Look at all those people."

"So what?"

"Oh, nothing," Barbara said. "I don't mind pulling up in front of all those people, getting out of the car with a ghostly young man who clearly has been sick all over himself, putting my snow skis on my shoulder, and walking into a tropical hotel. Why should I mind?"

"Okay." Fletch started to get out of the taxi. "Stay here. I'll send you out a poached egg."

"Either we're going to end up in a Kenyan jail," Barbara said, following him, "or an asylum for the insane."

"Pay the driver, Barbara. You've got the money."

"I'll tip him," Barbara said, "asking him to forgive us and forget us."

In fact, the big doorman took the skis out of the trunk, brought them into the lobby, and stood them up against the wall as if this were something he did hourly.

A few people on the veranda looked up and nodded at Fletch and Barbara.

In the people's eyes was little more than mild curiosity.

"Hello?"

There was a hesitation. "Is this Mr. Fletcher?"

"Is this Mr. Fletcher, too?" Fletch answered.

There was another pause. "My name's Carr. I'm a friend of your father's. Are you all up there?"

"All who?" Fletch asked. "Up where?"

"Is your father with you? With you and your wife, in your room?"

"I haven't seen him," Fletch said. "Ever."

"Oh. He told me we'd all meet here, on Lord Delamere's Terrace. For a drink. Rather think the old boy wanted me along for moral support, don't you know. I understand the situation. Father and son meeting for the first time."

Barbara was in the shower.

"More than I do, I expect."

Fletch had opened the knapsacks, gotten his shaving kit out.

"Well, I've got a table on the terrace. He'll turn up."

Slanted along the wall, propped against the windows, were the two pairs of snow skis. Outside the window, brilliant flowers were everywhere.

"I'll come down," Fletch said. "How will I know you?"

"Well, we'll be two proper-looking gentlemen, I trust, with drinks in front of our faces, all eyes on the front door of the hotel."

Fletch chuckled. "Okay. But I'll be a few minutes. We've spent the last several months on airplanes and you won't want to recognize me if I don't shave and shower."

"Right," Carr said. "We'll look for someone clean."

✦✦✦✦✦✦✦✦✦✦✦✦✦✦✦

"Did I hear the phone?" Barbara came out of the bathroom. Her head and torso were wrapped in towels.

"Yes." Shirt off, Fletch was going into the bathroom with his shaving kit.

"Was it your father?"

"No."

"Was it the police?"

"Why would it be? A friend of my father's, someone I guess my father wants present at the meeting for moral support. They'll be waiting for us downstairs on that veranda."

"Why didn't your father make the call?"

"He's not here yet. Barbara!"

"Yes, darling?"

"If we're to be married—"

"We were married. We are married."

"— either I'll have to grow a beard or be able to see in the mirror so I can shave."

"You told me I had first dibs on the shower."

"Why steam up the room? Why shower with the door closed?" There was a phone extension in the bathroom. "What century do you belong to, anyway? Why ever shower with the door closed?"

"The air's very dry here. See?" She reached her hand into the bathroom, closed her fingers, and threw the steam out. "All gone."

"I look lousy," he said, shaving.

"Yes," she said solemnly. "I was trying to spare you that view of yourself."

"Yeah, yeah."

"How do you feel?"

"I'm no more jet-lagged than you are. We'll live through the day."

"I can go down and say you're sick. You can meet these . . . your father, tomorrow."

"Why do that?"

"One shock to your system at a time. Isn't that what Aristotle said?"

"Aristotle said, 'The roast lamb is very good today.' "

"You're so contemporary."

When he came out of the shower, Barbara was still in her towels but there were clothes all over the room. Ski clothes. Sweaters. Ski boots. Ski goggles. Gloves. A kit of ski wax.

Barbara looked perplexed.

"Where are my clothes?" Fletch asked.

"In the laundry."

"What laundry?"

"A man came to the door and said he wanted clothes for the laundry so I gave him yours."

"Very generous of you."

"Mine, too. Everything we were wearing on the plane."

"Do I have any other clothes? I mean, to wear?"

"No," she said. "Neither do I. Apparently not." She waved her hand around the room. "Ski clothes."

"Not even jeans?"

"I told Alston I wasn't going to see you in jeans on our honeymoon. Or sneakers. Just ski clothes."

"Great."

He sat on the edge of the bed. Feet still on the floor, he lowered his back onto the bed. He was completely surrounded by ski clothes.

"You are still wet," she said.

"I won't catch cold."

She took off her torso towel. She wiped him down lightly, just once, from his shoulders to his ankles.

"You missed the soles of my feet."

"Raise your legs," she said. "Seeing everything else is up."

She knelt. He put his knees over her shoulders.

"Maypole," she said. "Flagpole. Tower of London." She was waving it back and forth. "There's nothing quite like it. Rigid, yet flexible."

"Millions of things just like it, so I hear."

"This is the one I've got ahold of."

"Right. That's the one."

"What will I do with it?" she asked.

"As you will. I can always grow another."

"Mmmmmm."

"My father . . ."

++++++++++++++

"My sneakers?" he asked.

"I gave them to the laundry man. I doubt you'll get them back."

Fletch stood in the middle of the room, dripping from a second shower.

"They'll be crocked by now." She was lying on some ski clothes on the floor, still looking at the ceiling.

"Who?"

"Your father and his friend. They'll be relaxed. You're relaxed."

"I figured he could wait."

Barbara rolled on her side and put her head on the palm of her hand. She bent one knee. "You look much better now. Your color has come back."

"Barbara, I have to meet my father, for first the time, dressed in ski clothes, in equatorial Africa. Powder blue or rich yellow?"

"Wear your blue. It's sort of a formal occasion."

"Ski boots!"

"Am I coming downstairs with you?"

"What do you think?"

"I think I could try to call my mother. She must be worried silly. I was supposed call her—how many days ago?—from Colorado!"

"Maybe I should meet him first myself. No distractions."

"No moral support?"

"My morals don't need support." He was pulling on nylon, formfitting, powder-blue ski pants.

"She's probably been bothering the airlines, the police, hospitals, the ski lodge. She must be frantic."

"I'm sorry. I should have asked Alston to call her."

"What sense would he have made? 'Hello, Mrs. Ralton. Fletch took your daughter to Africa. Said something about the white slave trade.'" She rolled onto her back. "Oh, God. What am going to say? 'Hi, Mom. The snow here is not all that great for skiing. We're in Africa.'"

"Is one of these sweaters at least lightweight?"

"Wear the red one."

"It looks hot."

"Roll up the sleeves. 'We missed doing what we said we were going to do by two whole continents and one huge ocean!'"

"Just tell her you're all right."

Keeping her legs straight, she raised them off the floor and held them, tightening her stomach muscles. "You're not going to talk to the police?"

He was stomping into his ski boots. "One thing at a time. As you just said."

" 'Hey, Mom! You know those aquamarine shorts of mine? Could you send them to Nairobi?' How's that for starters?"

"Sounds good." He clicked his boots shut and knelt on the floor. He leaned over and kissed Barbara.

She ran her hand along the inside of his leg. "Ummm. You feel good, even with pants on."

"The customs official thought they felt good, too."

"Strange customs."

At the door, he said, "You'll come down in a while?"

She rolled onto her stomach. "Sure. What did I say?"

" 'Don't be disappointed'?"

She winked at him. "You got it, babe."

There was only one proper-looking gentleman with a drink in front of his face, eyes on the front door of the hotel, when Fletch appeared on Lord Delamere's Terrace in ski boots, powder-blue ski pants, red sweater (sleeves rolled up), and sunglasses. At least there was only one proper-looking gentleman with drink in front of his face, eyes on the front door of the hotel, who gulped at the sight.

Others glanced and continued chatting.

That man began to rise, so Fletch went over to him.

The man held out his hand. "I'm Carr. The four-door model."

Shaking hands, Fletch said, "My father not here yet?"

"Can't think what happened to him." The man sat down again. His beer glass was half empty. It was a round table, with four chairs. Fletch sat across from him. Carr said, "You're a dazzler. Absolutely a dazzler. Is that what they wear in America these days?"

"When they're skiing."

At a table near them sat two paunchy men in short safari suits, balding, florid-faced, wearing competitive handlebar moustaches. At another table sat a woman in black, with a black picture hat. The man with her was in a double-breasted blue blazer, white shirt, and red tie. His hair was brilliantined. Jammed around another table were six students, male and female, black and white, jabbering excitedly, dressed in cutoffs and T-shirts. Two businessmen, briefcases on the floor beside them, talked earnestly at another table. Their white shirt cuffs and collars were between the perfectly matching blackness of their skins and suits. Many tables away three women sat together in brilliantly colored saris. Almost everyone else on the terrace was dressed in long or short khakis.

Carr asked, "Do you play guitar?"

"No," Fletch answered. "No talents."

Carr himself was dressed in khaki shorts, long khaki stockings, a short-sleeved khaki shirt. He was a solidly built middle-aged man with big knees, big forearms, big chest, and not too much gut. His hair was thinning, sandy. Even though his skin was deeply tanned, there was a light sunburn on top of it, and a few freckles on top of the burn. His hands were large, strong, heavily callused. His eyes were perhaps the clearest Fletch had ever seen.

"How do you like the Norfolk?" Carr asked.

"It seems authentic," Fletch said. "Perhaps the most authentic place I've ever been."

Carr chuckled. "I expect it is. In the old days, you know, the cowboys would come in so dusty and thirsty they'd ride their horses straight into the bar. The bar used to be through there in those days." He pointed to a blocked-off door. "Now that's a posh dining room. They'd be so dehydrated half a drink would make them looped, and they'd start shootin' the place up." He chuckled again. "I've been thrown out of here more times than I can recall."

"I bet." Fletch doubted it.

"Red, white, and blue."

Fletch looked down at his powder-blue pants and red sweater. "What's white?"

"You are."

"Oh, yeah. I forgot."

A young waiter said to Fletch, *"Jambo."*

"Jambo. Habari?"

"Habari, bwana?"

"Mzuri sana."

"Good God!" Carr said. "You speak swahili?"

"Why not?" Fletch checked his watch. "I've been here two and a half hours."

Carr gave Fletch a long look. Then he said to the waiter, *"Beeri mbili, tafahadhali."* He felt his glass. *"Baridi."*

Very carefully, Fletch said, *"Baridi."*

Laughing, Carr said, "You're a dazzler!" The waiter went away. "Americans never used to make an effort at languages."

Fletch looked across Harry Thuku Road to Nairobi University. "Does my father speak Swahili?"

"Oh, yes. Plus God knows what else. Has to, you see, flying small planes around the world. Here, ninety percent of the people speak English, ninety percent Swahili, and ninety percent speak at least one other, tribal language."

"What are you?" Fletch asked.

"What do you mean?"

"You could be English, American, South African, I suppose, Australian, from the way you sound."

"Not Austrylian," Carr said. "Not Austrylian. That takes too much bloomin' work. I'm Kenyan. Turned in a British passport for a Kenyan passport, and never regretted it. Live here awhile, and you're apt to sound like anything, I suppose. A cosmopolitan wee place."

"You're a pilot?"

"Still flying, as they say."

"'The man who appeared at my wedding, last Saturday, said nothing, but handed me the package with the tickets in it to come here was probably a pilot, yes?" Fletch was hot. The red sweater was prickling his skin. "He was a little guy, dressed in khaki, a blue tie."

"The international brotherhood of bush pilots."

"Where else have you flown?"

"Latin America, India. Some in the States. Other places in Africa."

"Smuggle?"

"That's not my business."

"Does my father?"

"That's not his business, either."

The waiter brought the beer.

Fletch said, "Thanks, *bwana*."

Carr smiled. He put his half-empty glass of beer onto the waiter's tray.

"How is my father?" Fletch asked.

Carr looked across the road. "We've all seen better days."

"He must be rich."

"Why do you say that?"

"Tickets here, for two, plus a thousand bucks, this hotel. That's a lot."

"Not over a lifetime. Have you ever had anything else from him?"

"No."

"Did you come here only because you thought he might be rich?"

"No. I was 'mildly curious.' "

"He's not rich."

"How do you suppose he knew I was getting married? Exact time, odd place . . . I barely made it myself."

Carr seemed to be studying his rough hands. "I suspect your father's been hearing from you all your life."

"Not from me."

"Hearing of you. I've seen pictures of you."

"Of me?"

"In a school yard. Walking along a street. In a football jersey. On a beach."

"All those dirty old men taking pictures of me."

"Pilot friends, I expect."

Fletch grinned. "And all these years I thought it was because I was so pretty."

"I take it you've never seen a picture of him?"

"No."

"What were you told?"

"I was allowed to think he was dead. He was declared dead, legally, when I was in the second year of school. I didn't know until last Saturday that my mother has always allowed for the possibility that he is alive. I guess she didn't want me to go off on some half-baked father search, you know, only to be disappointed."

Carr's eyes opened wider. He shook his head. "Absolutely," he said, "this has to be Mrs. Fletcher."

Fletch looked around.

Outside the door of the hotel stood Barbara, in ski boots, powder-blue ski pants, and a red sweater, sleeves rolled up.

"Three rabbits," Carr said to the waiter, "and I guess a beer for the lady."

"Rabbit," Barbara said softly. "Americans don't eat rabbits."

Carr had said they might as well have lunch.

After he ordered, Carr was interrupted by a man who came by the table. There was a brief introduction. The man and Carr talked about flying some glass specimen boxes to Kitale.

"This isn't your father?" Barbara whispered.

"A friend of his. Another pilot. Name of Carr. First name unknown."

"Where's your father?"

"He doesn't know. I think he's rather embarrassed. He's here as moral support, and the old man isn't here at all. He's trying to be very nice."

The conversation about glass specimen boxes was ending.

"Peter Rabbit," Barbara said. "Peter Cottontail. The Easter Bunny. 'What's up, Doc?' "

Carr said to Fletch, "My first name is Peter. People call me Carr."

"Peter."

"I can't eat Peter Cottontail," Barbara said.

Carr said, "What?" as does a man who suffers some permanent hearing disability.

"Where's Fletch's father?" Barbara said.

Carr looked at the entrance in obvious pain. "I wish I knew."

"Isn't there someplace you can call him?"

"This isn't Europe," Carr said. "The States. When a person goes missing here, it's not likely he's standing next to a phone."

"I called my mother," Barbara said to Fletch.

"What did you tell her?"

"I said, 'I'm in Nairobi, Kenya, East Africa, on my honeymoon with Fletch darling, I am very well, and sorry if you were worried when I didn't call you from Colorado.' "

"That's the thing," Carr said. "You can make a transworld call from here easier than you can call across the street."

"What did she say?"

"She thought I was joking. Then she said, 'Is that *boy* you married ever where he's supposed to be when he's supposed to be?' Then she said, 'There's some trick to everything he does. You can't live your life that way, Barbara.' "

Carr was trying to watch Fletch's eyes through Fletch's sunglasses.

Fletch put his sunglasses on the table.

"She said I should come home instantly and divorce you."

"Are you going to?"

"I was going to have lunch first. But rabbit?"

"Don't make a point in looking," Carr said, "but there's a man entering you mustn't miss."

The man went by the table like an aircraft carrier. He was six feet eight or nine inches tall and weighed nearly three hundred pounds. His head was a great, bald nose cone. He and Carr exchanged nods.

He sat at a table near the railing, back to the daylight, facing the entrance. He took a newspaper out and flattened it on the table.

Instantly, a waiter brought him a bottle of beer and a glass.

"He usually doesn't show here until about four o'clock in the afternoon," Carr said.

"Who is he?" Fletch asked.

Carr hesitated. The waiter was putting their plates in front of them. "His name is Dawes. Dan Dawes."

"What does he do?"

Barbara examined her plate. "They don't look like rabbits."

"He teaches high school."

"I'll bet his students call him 'Bwana.' "

"I daresay," Carr said.

Barbara put her knife into what was on her plate. "Cheese."

"Rarebit," Fletch said.

"They're cheese rabbits." Barbara began to eat happily.

The waiter was gone.

"He shoots people," Carr said. "At night. Almost always at night."

Barbara choked.

"Bad people, of course. Villains. Some say he does it for the police. He kills people the police can't get sufficient evidence against to bring to trial; people the police feel aren't worth the expense of a trial, and jail, or hanging."

"He just goes out and shoots people?"

"A blast from a .45 through the back of the head. Always very neat."

Barbara's eyes were bulging out of her head. "And he teaches school?"

"High school math."

Barbara looked at Fletch. "Is he the man—"

"Shut up, he said kindly," Fletch said.

As they ate, Fletch kept glancing at the huge man studying his newspaper. His bald head was as big as a boulder one would have to drive around.

Carr said, "You work for a newspaper?"

"Yes."

"That's nice. What particular abilities do you need for that?"

"Strong legs."

"And what do you get out of it?"

"A hell of an obituary."

Eating with delicate manners, the man with the rough hands asked Barbara, "And you?"

"I've been working in a boutique. Selling jodhpurs."

"Jodhpurs? My word, you Americans dress funny."

As they were finishing eating, Carr said, "How do you two feel?"

"Hot," Barbara said.

Fletch pulled at his sweater. "Hot."

"It's not hot, you know," Carr said. "You're at five thousand feet altitude."

Fletch said, "The slopes are dry, though. Definitely you need snow."

"I mean, how do you feel, jet lag and all?"

Barbara said, "Numb."

"We're determined to live through the day," Fletch answered. "Otherwise, we'll never adjust."

Carr thought a moment. "Seeing your dad doesn't appear to be appearing . . . How ought I say that? You write for a newspaper."

"He's not here," Fletch said. "And it's not news."

"I have some private business this afternoon, out in Thika." Suddenly there was even more red in Carr's face. "You both seem open enough. I mean, you're open to the fact that there is a language called Swahili, and you might pick up a few words." Barbara was watching Carr closely, wondering what he was talking about. "Private business. An odd sort of appointment. Well," he sighed. "Your dad seems to have missed this appointment, and I don't mean to miss mine." He scratched his ear. "With a witch doctor."

"A witch doctor," Fletch repeated.

"A witch doctor," Barbara repeated.

"I have a problem." Carr wasn't looking at them. "I'm not having much luck with something. There's a question I might as well ask."

Barbara said to Fletch, "A witch doctor."

"Sounds interesting," Fletch said.

Carr looked at his watch. "No point your hanging around here for Fletch to show up. I mean, the other Fletch. You might as well come with me. Take a ride through the suburbs of Nairobi."

"Are you sure we won't be in the way?" Fletch asked.

Carr laughed. "No, I'm not. But what's life without risk?"

Barbara said to Fletch, "I think if that other Fletch shows up, we don't particularly want to be here. Right now."

Carr skidded back in his chair. "I'll get the Land-Rover. It will only take a minute. It's over by the National Theater."

13

"Hurry up," Barbara said. "I want to do something."

They ran up the stairs at the back of the lobby.

"What?"

On the second floor they walked along a sun-dotted courtyard in which there was a Japanese garden.

"Get these clothes off me."

"Barbara, there isn't time. We kept this nice man waiting long enough this morning. He sat there sipping only half a beer while we screwed around."

"Will you tell Carr about what you saw this morning at the airport?"

"I was thinking of it." Fletch fitted their key to the lock. *"Witch doctor!?"*

In their room, all their clothes had been put away.

On the bureau was a pair of new sneakers. Next to them was a note.

Dear Mr. Fletcher:

Instantly your sneakers were damaged beyond repair in the wash so we have replaced them.

With apologies,
The Management
Norfolk Hotel

"My holey sneakers! How embarrassing!"

Barbara read the note over his shoulder. "How sweet!" She had a pair of scissors in her hand. "You're right. How embarrassing."

"What are you doing?"

"Take 'em off."

"Take what off?"

"I can't stand being in these clothes. I can't stand seeing you in those clothes. We can't go around on the equator dressed like this."

"My wife is attacking me with a scissors! We haven't been married a week!"

"Take your pants off or I'll cut them where you stand!"

"Help! Dan Dawes! Save me! There's a villain in my room!"

14

In the bright, midday sunlight, the shamba was country quiet.

Fletch and Barbara stood aside, along the stick fence inside the enclosure.

Carr, his big, rough hands looking useless hanging at his sides, stood in front of the witch doctor.

She sat on the ground in the doorway of her dung and thatch house. Her legs, wrapped in a black, thigh-length skirt, were straight and flat on the ground before her. Her feet were bare. There was a red Turkish cap on her head.

Her husband, in threadbare shorts, threadbare suit coat, no shirt, barefooted, sat on a low stool to her side, facing her, utterly attentive to her.

Together, the ancient couple did not weigh as much as one hundred pounds.

Across the enclosure there were three young men, late teenagers, dressed only in tawdry shorts, distantly present. Two were swaying drunk. The eyes of the third shone across the courtyard, attentive, alert.

The old lady witch doctor had drawn in white chalk a rectangle around her in the dirt, even over the dark little rug at her side. She had put white chalk dabs on each of her temples.

Then she had sung a nonmelodic song, prayer, incantation.

Her husband handed her a narrow-necked vase. Again and again, she would shake a few beads out of the vase into her hand, study them, flip them onto the dark rug, scatter them and regroup them with her fingers, watching how they came together. She would murmur a bit, sing a bit, gather the beads up, put them back in her vase, shake it, start over again.

The husband watched everything she was doing with reverent attention.

A clucking chicken crossed the enclosure.

Carr hadn't said much on the ride to Thika.

He had been waiting for them outside the hotel in his Land-Rover. He smiled when he saw Barbara and Fletch now in shiny powder-blue shorts, Fletch in thick ski socks and white new sneakers, his sweater cut from armpits to waist, sleeves cut off. Barbara was in one of Fletch's T-shirts and her rubber sandals. "That looks better," Carr said.

They stopped at an inn outside Nairobi called the Blue Post and had a cup of soup in a garden overlooking a short waterfall. "This soup cures all," Carr said. "Upset stomach. Broken heart. Although not traditional, probably even jet-lag. Very special here. Made of bones." He waved at the hills behind him. "Various animals. Boiled bones. Herbs. God knows what." It was a soup that puckered the throat. Fletch did feel better after drinking it.

Bouncing along the hard-top road, Carr missed the turning. He had to back up, half off the road, half on. Everywhere, along every road they had been on, besides the cars and trucks, there was a heavy traffic of people walking, both sides, going both ways, mostly people dressed in dark, cheap pants and shirts, dresses, many barefooted; always a few schoolchildren in uniform shorts and shoes, socks, shirts, and incongruous sweaters. Many times, Fletch noticed, there would be a man walking with a child or children. Carr turned onto a dirt track that wound through a field of standing corn.

Completely invisible from the road, thirty meters inside this cornfield was a little village, a half-dozen well-spaced dung and conically thatch-roofed houses, each separated by its own thick stick fencing.

The witch doctor appeared and took her position sitting in the doorway as they arrived. This was a genuine appointment. Carr gave Barbara and Fletch a look indicating they should stand aside in silence. He stood in front of the old lady.

Suddenly, the third young man, the one with the lively eyes, strode across the enclosure in a full-blown gait that could carry him across the world. He stood between Barbara and Fletch. They made room for him. He faced Carr and the witch doctor. Then he sat down on his heels.

In a moment, he tugged Fletch's ski sock.

Fletch looked down.

"I'm James," the young man said. "Get down."

Fletch bent his knees but could not sit on his heels. Not for long. He sat cross-legged on the ground.

Barbara sat cross-legged, too.

Seeing this, James changed his position so that he, too, was sitting cross-legged. One of his knees was on Barbara's leg, the other on Fletch's.

Fletch jerked his thumb at his wife. "Barbara." He pointed his thumb at himself. "Fletch."

James's eyes widened. He stared into Fletch's eyes and then looked away. He gave Fletch the whole song, all five notes: "Oh, I see. Sorry."

"Say what?"

"I know of your father." James rushed on. "The reason I told you to sit down, you see," James said softly, "is because these things take a long time." He said to Barbara, "You must be careful not to get sunbite."

Barbara looked confused. She was against the fence. There was no place for her to move.

Whispering, James said, "Do you know what the man asked her?"

Carr had said something to the witch doctor after she had put the chalk around her and on her temples.

Fletch said, "I heard, but I didn't understand."

"He said he is trying to find something. He wants her to tell him where it is."

"Why did she put the white marks on her temples?" Barbara asked.

James looked at her as if she had asked if the sun rises in the east everywhere. "So she can communicate through the gods on Mount Kenya with your ancestors."

Fletch said, "Oh, I see."

"The white is the snow."

"*That's* the snow," Barbara said.

Sitting against the stick fence in the dirt under an equatorial sun, Fletch asked, "Has she ever seen real snow?"

"I doubt it. She's reading the beads. Five beads is for man, three for woman, two for house. Something like that. I don't know. Each bead means something different. It's all very complicated."

"It must take a long time to learn," Barbara said.

"Learn," James said. "Yes. But, you see, she is a witch doctor."

"You mean, she doesn't have to learn?"

"Yes, much," James said. "But you can't learn, if you haven't the ability."

James pulled a sun-bleached hair out of Fletch's leg. He looked at it closely between his fingers in the sunlight. Still holding it, he looked at Barbara's legs. Examining the hair again, he said, "It must be funny to be not black."

Fletch heard Barbara saying, "You are a blackness I've never seen before. You're so very black the way some people are so very white."

"I have no white blood," James said. "Probably in England or America or wherever you come from all the black people you see aren't black at all. They have white blood. Do you like being white?"

"Well enough," Fletch said.

James blew the hair off his fingers. "I haven't decided whether it's better being black or white."

"Is James your real name?" Fletch asked.

"Why isn't it?"

"It's not an African name, is it?"

"Would you rather call me . . ." James seemed to be making up a name. ". . . Juma?"

"Sure. I don't care."

"That's fine," James said. "You've probably known another James somewhere before, and you shouldn't confuse me with him."

Barbara said, "Not likely, Jim-Bob."

Juma giggled. "The witch doctor just said to the man, 'You are looking for something you haven't lost.'"

There was a conversation going on so quietly over by the doorway Fletch was scarcely aware of it. "Did Carr agree?"

"Carr said it's a place he's looking for. It's been lost a long time."

Now Carr was leaning over the witch doctor.

The old woman put her cupped hands up to him.

Carr spit in her hands.

Fletch looked at the ground. "Maybe I should ask her where my father is."

"Your father's not lost," Juma said. "He's here in Kenya. Fletch. I know him."

"What do you know about him?"

"He flies planes. I've seen him. I've seen Carr before, too. I get everywhere."

Barbara said, "Shhh."

Juma whispered, "She said he'll find the place, but it will be difficult. The dead people there want him to find it, so they will be remembered." He listened a moment. "She said he must go far, far south where there are hills and look for a river."

Carr looked around at Fletch. His face beamed with vindication.

"Oh, wow," Barbara said. "Mumbo jumbo."

Fletch asked, "How old are you?"

Again Juma seemed to take the time to invent something. "Thirty-seven."

Fletch said, "Okay."

Juma was listening intently. He put his hand on Fletch's knee. "She's talking about you." The witch doctor was looking at her beads on the little rug, rolling them back and forth. She appeared to be talking to them. "She's asking why don't you come forward."

Forehead creased, Carr was looking at Fletch. Juma pushed him. "Get up. Go forward. She's saying something to you."

Fletch got up. He dusted off the seat of his pants.

He stood in front of the tiny witch doctor.

Carr said, "She wants to know why you haven't talked to her."

"No disrespect," Fletch said. "Right. Where's my father?"

Carr started to speak to the old woman. Instantly she began to speak, not to Fletch but to the beads she was rolling around the rug.

When she paused, Carr said, "She says you have no question, but something you must say, or it will be worse for you."

"What will get worse?"

The witch doctor was continuing to make her little noises.

"She says you must speak to her. You are carrying a box of rocks? which will get heavier and heavier until your legs break."

"I have strong legs."

"Do you know what she's talking about?"

"Maybe."

"She says you must drop this box of rocks or go away, as she does not want to see your legs shatter."

Fletch looked across the enclosure at the two teenagers swaying, dizzy-eyed drunk in the sunlight. He looked at Barbara and Juma sitting together against the fence like schoolchildren born and bred together. He looked down at the little old lady sitting in the dirt in the doorway of her dung house.

He looked into Carr's face.

Fletch said, "They're my rocks."

++++++++++++++

Fletch was the first one out of the enclosure, to spare the witch doctor the sight of his legs shattering.

Fletch hit his head against a thick branch forming an arch over the gate.

Juma said the two-note song: "Sorry."

Rubbing his head, Fletch said, "Why are you apologizing? I walked into it."

Juma said, "I'm sorry you bonked your noggin."

Barbara came through the gate, sunburned.

Carr exited, looking bemused, if not bewitched.

They went up the track to the Land-Rover.

Swaying, the two young men were fumbling with the gate.

Fletch said to Juma, "Your two friends are pretty drunk."

" 'Friends'?" Juma did not look at them. He did not look at Fletch. He looked deep into the standing corn.

Juma frowned, but said nothing.

"No, I don't know him." Carr smiled. "I thought he was a friend of yours."

On the dance floor at the Shade Hotel, Juma was break-dancing with some paid-for performers. It was early in the evening and only a few of the tables in the yard had people at them. The performers seemed to be showing Juma a few things, and Juma seemed to be showing them a few things. A tape machine at the edge of the stage/dance floor was playing "Get Out of Town" loudly.

"He just got into the car with us," Barbara said. They were at a little wooden table under an umbrella. "First he said his name is James. Then he said we could call him Juma."

Carr said, "He probably just wants a ride back to Nairobi."

Carr had gone across the yard to the barbecue pit and ordered their dinners. A waitress brought three beers.

Fletch said, "I asked him how old he is and he said thirty-seven."

"He is thirty-seven," Carr said.

They watched Juma on the stage/dance floor spinning like a top on the muscles of his left shoulder.

"There are two rainy seasons a year here," Carr said. "The short rains and the long rains. Ask someone how old he is, and he'll tell you how many rainy seasons he has behind him. In Juma's case, it would be thirty-seven. That means he's eighteen and a half years old."

Fletch said, "Oh, I see." He was getting the three little notes nearly right.

On their way from the witch doctor's shamba to the Shade Hotel, Carr had driven them on a detour through Karen. They had stopped at Karen Blixen's, that is, Isak Dinesen's farm, or what's left of it. Not a tarted-up tourist attraction yet, the low stone house and a few acres adjoin a business school. They had gotten out of the Land-Rover and walked around, under the trellis, through the roots and trunks of the great trees in back.

Barbara and Fletch had sat for a moment on the stone arrangements near the back door where Karen Blixen had held court with *her people* and maybe did some of her writing about them.

"Dinesen, Hemingway, Roark," Carr said. "That was all light-years ago, in African time."

"Time, space." Juma started back to the Land-Rover. "They were always light-years away from Africa, anyway."

In the deepening dusk at the table in the yard of the Shade Hotel, Carr said, "You must be aware of what time it is, too. You're on the equator. The sun rises at roughly seven each morning and sets at roughly seven each night, year-round. Sunrise is the beginning of the day, naturally, and sunset the beginning of the night. So if someone says he'll see you at three tomorrow, he might mean ten o'clock in the morning. Ten might be five o'clock in the afternoon. Five tomorrow night is midnight."

Fletch said, "Oh, I see."

"It is through such simple misunderstandings," Carr said, "that cultures clash."

The waitress brought them a large plate of cooked meat and a bowl of rice. She placed three paper plates on the table.

Carr took a piece of the meat in his fingers. With it he lifted rice from the bowl into his mouth.

"Shouldn't we ask Juma if he wants something to eat?" Barbara asked.

Carr said, "He doesn't want to eat now."

Barbara raised her eyebrows. "Say what, *bwana*?"

"Traditionally, people here eat only one meal a day, at nine or ten o'clock at night, after it cools down. A very high-protein meal, if they can get it. They believe eating during the heat of the day makes you sick, fat, and lazy." Carr looked around him at the few other people at that early hour. "Some come to the city, of course, put on polyester clothes, take to eating three meals a day, and in no time they took just as chubby and pasty as your average New Yorker."

Watching him dancing, Barbara said, "Juma is not chubby and pasty."

"So," Carr said. "He doesn't want to eat now."

Eating the meat and rice with his fingers, Fletch asked Carr, "What are you looking for?"

"Beg pardon?"

"For what are you looking? Or shouldn't I ask? At Thika, Juma was translating for us. He said you told the witch doctor you are looking for a place. You asked her where it is."

"Oh, that," Carr said.

"Private business," warned Barbara.

Fletch shrugged. "No one ever has to answer a question."

"No one ever has to ask a question, either," Barbara said."

"I'm a reporter."

"You're not working now."

"May the searchlight of the free press never darken," said Fletch.

In the glow of the kerosene lamp on the table, Carr's face looked more red than usual.

"The witch doctor was fascinating," Barbara said. "Thank you for taking us. You said people working in holistic medicine now are taking an interest in the witch doctor generally . . ."

Suddenly, Carr said, "I'm looking for a Roman city."

"Huh?" Fletch asked.

"Good!" exclaimed Barbara. "Finally an answer to one of your impertinent questions made you almost swallow your teeth!"

"Here?"

Carr nodded. "In East Africa."

Barbara sighed.

"Hell of a long walk from home," Fletch said. "Through Egypt, the Sudan, Ethiopia . . . ? How could they supply themselves through thousands of miles of desert?"

"The Arabians did," Barbara said. "It can't be all desert."

"Down the Red Sea," Carr said. "Into the Somali Basin."

"By boat."

"The reason people have always doubted it," Carr said, "is because once you get into the Somali Basin the southwest winds and currents are strongly against one."

"So?"

"So," Carr said. "They rowed."

"Hello of a long row."

"Difficult, I admit. But the Romans did difficult things."

"What would they want here?" Barbara asked.

"Spices. Minerals. Gems."

"The Romans conquered the known world," Fletch said. "This world was unknown."

"Right," said Carr. "Kenya would be farther than anyone has ever believed the Romans traveled."

"A Roman city in Kenya," Barbara said.

"Kenya is as far from Rome as is New York," Fletch said.

"The Romans came to America," Barbara said.

"They didn't build cities."

"No," said Barbara. "They ate lobsters and either died or went home. Typical tourists."

"I don't think the Romans ever went to America on purpose," Carr said. "They got blown there by mistake. No one from Europe ever got blown to East Africa by mistake. I think the Romans came here, settled here, and were here for a very long time."

"If Barbara will forgive another impertinent question," Fletch said, "what makes you think so?"

"To be honest," Carr said, "there is currently a small rumor circulating that some documentary evidence of there having been a Roman city on the East African coast south of the equator has turned up in London. That's all I know about it: there's a rumor. But long before I heard this rumor, I have believed it. Always."

"Why?"

"The Masai." Carr sat back in his chair. "How can you observe the Masai and possibly believe the Romans weren't here?"

Fletch shook his head as if to clear it.

"Right," Carr said. "There is a tribe called the Masai. Bantu origins, cousins of the Samburu. The Masai roam the south, the Kenyan-Tanzanian border; the Samburu the north. The Masai are a warrior tribe. They carry spears. Traditionally, they carry shields. They wear togas. Historically, Masai young men go through intensive training in the arts of war, to attain the rank of *moran*, warrior, including elaborate tests of courage. From what is known, the Masai were perfectly disciplined to use complicated, sophisticated military formations and tactics. So perfect were they as a military force that they succeeded in keeping the Western world, the white people, with their bows, arrows, crossbows, and gunpowder, out of inland East Africa until very nearly the beginning of the twentieth century. What finally made them retreat was the automatic rifle and the English railroad. The coast had been opened, Lamu, Malindi, Mombasa, fought over by the Arabians, Portuguese, whoever. But no one ever went inland, so terrified were they of the Masai."

Barbara picked gristle off her meat. "Why couldn't they have developed these military tactics on their own?"

"They could have," said Carr. "But some of their military tactics were appropriate only for urban areas. There weren't any urban areas for them to develop such tactics. And why, if they did develop these disciplines and tactics themselves, are these techniques, even their mode of dress, so similiar to the Romans?"

"Come on," Fletch said. "Why would an African tribe maintain a military discipline imposed on them by a foreign culture for over two thousands years?"

"Because," Carr answered, "the Masai are a very fragile people. Extremely tall. Extremely thin. Traditionally, they eat only meat, milk, and blood."

"Good God," said Barbara.

Carr smiled at her. "They produce the best-smelling sweat in the world."

"What?"

"Their perspiration smells beautiful. It's a heavy, dense, clean odor you could bottle and sell in your boutique."

"Masai Perspiration *parfum*." Barbara shook her head. "I don't think it would be a hit."

"The Masai are so brittle," Carr said, "they can never win in hand-to-hand combat. As soon as their ancient enemies, the Kĩkuyu, would penetrate the Masai's disciplined formations and go at them with their hands and feet, the Masai would lose. Maintaining this Roman militarism was their only way of surviving as a people for two thousand years."

Electronic music was blaring from the stage.

"In fact," added Carr, "the Masai are so brittle they have trouble bearing children. Over the centuries they have needed the women of other tribes. The Masai were not just militarily defensive, but these enormously tall, skinny people had to be militarily aggressive to survive."

"Whew." Fletch shook his head. "Witch doctors. A lost Roman city. Carr, you are a surprising fellow."

Carr shrugged. "It's just a hobbyhorse of mine. If anything works out, I might make a bit of a name for myself. It's so crazy anyway, I didn't mind going to a witch doctor about it. You never know what little thing might come out of traditional wisdom."

"Are you actually spending time and money looking for this place?" Barbara asked.

"Time and money. I have a camp set up. Sheila's there now."

"Is Sheila your wife?"

"Might as well be. Dear old thing's been with me years now."

Barbara looked shyly at him. "Has either of you a degree in anthropology, archaeology, anything?"

"Good heavens, no. Barely finished school. But to paraphrase the ignoramous regarding art, I'll know when I see something out of the ordinary."

Fletch smiled. "And is your camp in the south, in the hills, near a river?"

Carr nodded. "Exactly. Figured the Romans needed a certain altitude, a supply of fresh water, and a river big enough to give them access to, yet protection from, the sea."

Fletch pushed his chair back. "We won't tell anyone."

He couldn't imagine Frank Jaffe's reaction to such a story anyway. *Avalanches, mud slides, major earthquakes, airplane crashes, train wrecks, mass murders, acts of terrorism, airport bombings . . . Be sure and phone in, if you get any good stuff . . .*

Hello, Frank! I'm onto a search for a lost Roman city on the East African coast. One of my sources is the witch doctor of Thika . . .

Uh, Frank . . . ?

"Tell anybody you like," Carr said. "*Harambee.* All in good clean fun. Better than poaching elephant tusks."

"Go for it."

Carr smiled at Barbara. "I thought you'd prefer the goat to the beef."

Barbara said, "What goat?"

"Anytime you have a choice around here between goat and beef," Carr said, standing up, "choose the goat."

Barbara was looking at the empty plates. "I've been eating goat?"

"It's much more tender," Carr said, "than beef. Tastier, too."

"I've been eating goat? I ate Billy the Goat?"

Suddenly, Barbara looked ill.

++++++++++++++

On the dark sidewalk outside the Norfolk Hotel, Juma crossed his arms over his chest. His feet were planted far apart.

Carr had just driven away in the Land-Rover.

Juma said to Fletch: "At the shamba in Thika you said my friends were drunk."

"Sorry," Fletch said. "Didn't mean to insult your friends. They looked pretty drunk to me."

"How do you decide friends?"

Fletch said, "I don't care about drunkenness."

"How do you decide who is your friend? Is that something you decide about?"

"What?" Barbara asked.

"How can you decide someone is your friend without deciding everyone else is not your friend?"

"I'm not sure I understand," Fletch said.

"Do you decide who is your enemy? That's not the way things happen," Juma said.

"Oh, I see."

"Things just happen," Juma said. "When you first saw me, I was with those boys. They were drunk. I don't decide if they are my friends or not my friends. Maybe they are my enemies. How could you decide?"

Barbara shook her head. "I am very, very tired. I don't have to decide that."

Juma grabbed her arm. "That's right!"

"Barbara said something right?"

Juma looked all around. "Deciding everything like that, all the time, north, east, south, west, is very hard."

Barbara asked, "Do you mean difficult . . . ?"

". . . or harsh?" Fletch finished.

Juma turned and began walking away from them down the street. He waved. "Nice time!"

Watching him, Barbara asked, "Does he mean, *Have* a nice time . . . ?"

". . . or We *had* a nice time?" Fletch finished.

"I don't know." Barbara took Fletch's arm as they started into the hotel. "But he understands Fletch is your father . . . "

". . . and he's sorry."

Fletch had a funny line ready but, although he had used it before, he couldn't remember it. Instead, he said, "Hello?"

"Did you both sleep well?"

"So far." Fletch remembered the line. "Is this Fletch, too?"

" 'Fraid not. Carr here again."

"Oh." Fletch finally got his head off the pillow and rolled over. "There was a message waiting for us at the hotel when we got back last night. My father had been here during the afternoon."

"I'm sure he was, old chap."

"And that he'd call us in the morning."

"I'm sure he meant to."

"This is morning?" The window was filled with gray daylight. In the bed beside him, Barbara had not noticed.

"Shortly before eight of the clock, Nairobi time. To my surprise, I'm downstairs about to have breakfast. I only have an hour or so this morning."

"That's very nice . . ."

"Hate to awaken you this way, your first real day here, and all that. Your father called me a couple of hours ago. Something's come up, you see. If you could pull yourself together and join me for a cup of coffee, I could fly away with a sense of duty done."

"Something's happened to my father?"

"Yes."

"I'll be right down."

++++++++++++++

"The Kenyan coffee is quite pleasant but you might want to cut it with milk or hot water."

The waiter was pouring black coffee into Fletch's cup. Carr was finishing a large bowl of fruit.

He said, "The pineapple here is probably better than anywhere."

"Barbara will be right down."

"Yes."

There was a huge, round, beautiful breakfast buffet in the middle of the Lord Delamere dining room.

"What's up?" Fletch asked.

"The senior Fletcher called me about five-thirty this morning. It seems there's been a spot of trouble."

Carr was right. The coffee did need cutting. "What kind of trouble?"

"It seems that yesterday, the senior Fletch, doubtlessly nervous about your imminent arrival, began quaffing the local brew a bit early on."

"He got drunk."

"With the resultant loss of sense of time and place."

"Which is why he didn't show up."

"Sometime during the day, he's not sure just when, he found himself in an altercation at the Thorn Tree Café. Someone, he says, insulted the Queen."

"What Queen?"

"The Queen of England. Elizabeth Regina Twice."

"What does he care about the Queen of England? He's born and bred Montana."

"We all care about the Queen of England out here, old chap. She's very fond of Kenya. Been here twice."

Carr drew his knife across the surfaces of the two fried eggs the waiter had brought him. "What came up was his fist. He's aware of having done damage to two or three people, seems to remember the sounds of glass smashing, seeing one of those little tables in matchsticks on the ground, and of being very angry at a placating *askari*, although whether he actually hit him is something the senior Fletcher is trying to reason through this morning. Why don't you go get your fruit?"

"What's an *askari*?"

"A guard. Possibly a cop. It will make a difference when this matter comes to trial."

"He got into a bar fight."

"So he testifies."

"He was doing that sort of thing at age fifteen, or so my mother testifies."

"I'd give you a rhyming couplet about the boy in every man, but I never was that strong on Wordsworth."

"So where is he now, in jail?"

"Not yet. He's gone to ground to reconstruct his head and think things through. I had the discretion not to ask from where he was calling. He'll have to face the tune sooner or later, of course. Nairobi isn't like London or New York, you know. Everyone here knows who Fletcher is. On the other hand, people here didn't used to take this sort of bash-up all that seriously."

"Mother warned me he was apt to evade emotional moments."

"Did she? Is that what she said? How very kind of her. Understanding, I'd say."

"So why did he invite me here if it was going to be so upsetting for him?"

"Sometimes you don't know your *kanga* has a loose thread."

"Is that from Wordsworth?"

"Maybe. It makes a great deal of difference whether the *askari* he hit was a private watchman or a real policeman."

"You indicated yesterday the law is very strict here."

"Very. It has lost its sense of humor."

"Listen, Carr . . ."

"Why don't you get some breakfast? Fried eggs you have to order from the waiter."

"You probably know where my father is."

"Probably."

"Why don't I go to him now, get this confrontation over? Maybe I can even be a help to him."

"I've got a better idea. Why don't you fly up to Lake Turkana with me today? I've got to deliver a scientist up there. I'll be coming right back. You can have a swim. We can have lunch. Nile perch. Nice time."

"My father—"

"Put yourself in his shoes, Fletch. He's got a hell of a hangover. Probably a bloody nose. He's liable for arrest. Last thing anyone would want under such circumstances is for a dazzling kid who looks like he's never farted to come walking in offering aid and assistance, calling him *Daddy*."

"I've farted."

"Glad you heard it."

Fletch looked at the buffet. "Guess I'll get some breakfast."

"Breakfast," said Carr, "is the only fortification left to modern man."

++++++++++++++

While Fletch circumnavigated the breakfast buffet, he saw Barbara enter the room, kiss Carr on the cheek, and sit down.

On his plate Fletch placed pineapple, scrambled eggs, sausage, bacon, and toast. He also took a glass of orange juice.

"Just explaining to your wife," Carr said, "that the senior Fletcher is held up today by a sticky legal problem. Suggesting you both fly up to Turkana with me . . ."

"Nice of you . . ." Barbara's eyes were filled with questions.

"About a two-and-a-half-hour flight each way. Lake Turkana is very interesting. Used to be called the Jade Sea. Plenty of room in the plane. Carries eight passengers and there's only this one small scientist going. A Dr. McCoy. He won't mind at all."

Barbara said, "I'm a little sick of airplanes . . ."

Carr looked at his watch. "Trouble is, I have to be going. I told Dr. McCoy I'd be ready to take off at ten."

"You go, Fletch," Barbara said. "I really need a down day. There's a swimming pool somewhere here. I've never even looked in the aviaries in the courtyard yet."

"Sure you'll be all right?" Fletch was eating rapidly.

"If I get bored I can go walk around that mosque near here. I've never seen a real mosque."

"I'll get the car. You'll be out front in five minutes, Fletch?"

"Sure."

After Carr left the breakfast room, Barbara said, "Fletch, darling. There is something about your father that doesn't make sense."

Fletch drained his cup of the strong coffee. "We knew that before we arrived."

Barbara shoved Fletch away from the bathroom mirror. "Is this what life with you is going to be like?"

Fletch was brushing his teeth. "What do you mean?"

She put toothpaste on her own brush. "Always running away? Always being somewhere else?"

She already had changed into her swimsuit.

"Carr invited both of us," Fletch said. "You said you didn't want to come. You said you were sick of airplanes, want to spend the day resting by the pool."

"Lovely," Barbara said. "You fly me to East Africa, worry my mother frantic, then fly off into the bush, leaving me in some tropical hotel . . ."

"I agreed to go. I thought you would want to go, too."

"I said I wanted to stay here. I thought you'd say you wanted to stay here, too."

"Will you let me rinse my mouth? Please?"

Barbara stepped aside, but not much. "We got married. Big event in life. We flew halfway around the world, totally unprepared. Big event. To meet your father, for the first time, which should be a big event, except he decides he's got something better to do than meet us. Yesterday, you saw someone get stabbed to death in a bathroom. Big bloody event! And today you want to go flying off into the African bush to someplace we've never heard of, with someone we don't even know!"

"You losing your sense of humor?"

"When is enough enough for you? Can't you sit still a damned minute?"

"Okay," Fletch said. "I'll go downstairs and tell Carr I'm not going. We'll sit by the pool."

She had put the cap back on the toothpaste and placed the tube neatly on the counter.

Barbara turned and faced Fletch. "No. You go." Suddenly her tight fist, much smaller and harder than Fletch had realized, smashed into Fletch's stomach, low, just inside his right hipbone. "Take that with you."

Fletch lowered his head. He looked up at her. "No one's ever hit me there before."

"First time for everything."

Fletch walked into the hallway outside the bathroom. "I can't stay now."

"That's a nice excuse."

"Take it as you like it. See you at dinner."

"How's married life so far?" Carr drove the Land-Rover along the left-hand side of Harry Thuku Road.

Half a block from the Hotel Norfolk, on the left, just before the rotary, Fletch noticed a police station/jail.

After a moment, Fletch answered, "There's a difference between men and women."

"Yes," Carr said. "There is. Shall I sing you a few million songs about that? Never mind. You may have only one life to live." He shifted down.

"Okay. You know Barbara and I had a disagreement."

Of the men who walked along the road, many were with children.

A few raindrops appeared on the windshield.

"Hope Barbara's having a nice day by the pool," Fletch said.

"Never begrudge Africa its rain," Carr said. "We'll go a bit out of our way to have lunch at the fishing lodge on

Lake Turkana, which is nothing to write home about. But, before that, you can swim in their pool, which is."

"Which is what?"

"Something to write home about."

"How can a swimming pool be something to write home about?"

"You'll want a swim by the time we get there." Carr was smiling to himself.

Fletch noticed a dog-eared paperback on Carr's dashboard. *Murder by Rote.* By Josie Fletcher. Fletch picked it up. "You read my mother?"

"Her biggest fan. Have you read that one?"

Fletch was thumbing through the book. "How can I tell?"

"She must be a very sensible woman, your mother."

"Sensible?" Adjectives sometimes used to describe his mother always amazed Fletch. Sensible. Observant. Clever about clocks set wrong and dogs that don't bark. Practical. Wise. Logical. Adjectives used by her few fans. "Yes, she might notice if her house were on fire. But she'd probably finish writing her chapter before doing anything about it."

Carr shifted in his seat. "Have you seen her lately?"

"Last Saturday. The day I was married."

"Still, I gather, a woman, without much education, she's supported herself, and you, at a hard profession . . ."

"I appreciate it." Fletch tossed the book back onto the dashboard. "We had a good conversation. I really pinned her down about my father. My hearing from him forced the issue."

"Oh?" Carr cleared his throat. "What did she say about him?"

"She said she loved him. His disappearance left her in a state of permanent shock. She's been trying to solve mysteries ever since."

"Maybe the quality of a writer is determined by the universality of the mystery he's trying to solve."

Leaning against his door, right arm over the chair back, Fletch stared at Carr.

"A pilot has lots of time to think," Carr said, as if excusing himself. "Literally, his head is in the clouds. Why does human life take the forms it does? Families, friends . . . What are these institutions humans keep creating, destroying, and re-creating for ourselves? Religions, nations, families, businesses, clubs . . . What are they for? Given the uniqueness of life, how can one person purposely take the life of another, for any reason?"

"My mother supports herself by writing detective stories," Fletch said. "There's nothing mysterious about it."

They were stuck in traffic.

"What are we?" Carr mused.

Fletch said, "We are all mysteries waiting to be solved."

"Now you've got the beat." Carr beat out a little rhythm with his fingers on the steering wheel. "One has to think *something*." The traffic began to move. "Odd, though, that your mother never told you much about your father. She must be articulate."

"She really hasn't known all these years whether he's dead or alive."

"She had him declared dead?"

"She had to, to get on with her own life."

"Therefore you thought he was dead."

"Kids believe what they're told. When the courts say, 'Your daddy is dead,' the kid says, 'Okay. My daddy is dead. What's for lunch?'"

"What was for lunch?"

"Usually the question, 'How do you spell *hors d'oeuvres*?' My mother never could spell *hors d'oeuvres*. It's a wonder she kept serving 'em up in her books."

"All this is more of a suprise to you than I thought."

"You don't get used to not having a father. Then again, you do."

"Then someone comes along and says, 'Here's Papa!' "

"Where is Papa?"

Carr swung out to pass. "Walter Fletcher has screwed up."

"She also told me she never told me much about Walter because Walter wasn't there to defend himself."

Carr breathed a whistle through his teeth. "Nice lady."

"Sometimes, any news is better than no news."

"I'm not so sure." Carr turned left onto the airport road. "Barbara's not missing much of a trip. Too murky really to see the green hills of Africa. Still, she's getting her rest by the sunless pool. And your company is pleasant. I guess you're the one person in the world I don't have to worry about stealing *Murder by Rote* before I finish it."

"Carr?" Fletch banged his fist on the pilot's shoulder. Carr shoved the radiophone forward off his right ear. "There's a body down there. A man on the ground."

Carr leaned over Fletch and looked through the starboard window of the airplane. He dipped the right wing so he could see better. "So there is."

The naked man was lying on his side, far from any bush.

Carr said, "I was wondering what the vultures had found for themselves."

The circling birds had drawn Fletch's attention to the man on the ground.

They had flown about two hours northwest from Nairobi, over the White Hills and the eastern edge of Lake Naivasha. Looking down, Fletch had seen the enormous, white Djinn Palace at the edge of the lake.

Carr had pointed out the great gash in the land called the Rift Valley. "Someday, we're told," Carr shouted over the sound of the engine, "the Red Sea will come flooding down that rift. Hope I've got my waders on that day!"

Now, Fletch knew by the chart in his lap, they were somewhere east of the Loichangamata Hills. There were no shambas below them.

The scientist they were transporting to Lake Turkana, Dr. McCoy, had taken a backseat in the airplane. A little, very white man in a seersucker suit, wide-brimmed safari hat, and canvas bush boots, he coughed continuously and spat into his handkerchief frequently. He had not asked why Fletch was accompanying them to Lake Turkana on the doctor's chartered plane. He had not asked anything or said much.

Carr turned the plane and swooped lower over the figure on the ground.

As Carr did so, Fletch pointed out the body to McCoy in the seat behind him.

"Is he dead?" Fletch asked Carr.

"Look at the hyenas." Carr could not point while he was turning the plane again. "They're just waiting. And the vultures are waiting for the hyenas."

Carr was bringing the plane around to land near the man.

Leaning forward, McCoy said, "Leave him!"

Carr looked over his shoulder at him.

"He was left there to die," McCoy said.

"Ah, culture clash," Carr said, facing forward. "He's an anthropologist or something. I suppose he's right."

Carr was still making for a landing.

"I said, leave him!" McCoy shouted. "You're not to interfere with their nature!"

McCoy began coughing.

Carr turned his head so McCoy could hear him. "I haven't your education, McCoy. It's my nature I must sleep with!"

McCoy spat into his handkerchief.

Just after the wheels of the plane touched the ground, Fletch threw up the door next to his seat and held it open. Carr had taught him to do that, taking off from Wilson Airport, to rid the cockpit of the terrible, immediate heat on the ground.

++++++++++++++

"Poor bastard. He's been *pangaed*."

The man's skull was split open. Brain matter was visible.

There was the great patience of the nearly dead in the man's eyes as he watched Carr and Fletch approach.

"How can he be alive?" Fletch asked.

"Tough nut."

Carr haunched next to the man and spoke with him. The man answered slowly, from a parched throat, through a swollen tongue. He never closed his mouth completely.

McCoy stood coughing under the wing of the plane. He had only gotten out of the cockpit to get out of the heat.

Carr said, "He says he stole six goats."

"Honest of him to say so."

"They caught up to him, cut his head open with a machete, and left him to die." Carr looked at the birds circling above them. "To be eaten." He looked over to where some hyenas sat next to a bush. "Rude justice."

"Why did he tell you the truth? Why doesn't he say *he* was robbed or something?"

Carr stood up. "Under prevailing circumstances, vultures about to pluck out one's eyes, hyenas about to begin their feed on one by first cracking off one's hands and one's feet, one is probably well advised, happier, if you catch my drift, if one is honest with oneself as to how one fell victim to such circumstances."

"For six goats?"

"Nothing is more important than goats. They rank right up there with wives in the local economy." Carr stooped to look into the skull wound. He had brought a medical kit from the airplane. "In every way, goats are the scourge of the third world."

A little fresh blood continued to trickle onto the dried, crusted blood. Flies were everywhere over the wound and over the naked man. The flies walked on the man's eyeballs. They probed his nostrils. They walked along his lips and entered and exited his mouth.

"Why didn't they kill him?" Fletch asked. "Why leave him like this?"

"Having six goats stolen can ruin a family, for at least a generation."

Carr wrapped gauze around the man's head. "Just trying to hold his brains in. Although I guess I cleaned up worse things off the cockpit floor. There. Let's get him up."

As they lifted the man upright and began to walk/carry him between them to the airplane, the hyenas began to yell angrily. They paced up and down in protest, coming nearer.

"We're certainly upsetting nature," Carr said. "May God forgive me."

McCoy did nothing to help them lift the man onto the rearmost seat of the airplane. Carr buckled him in.

At no point did the man cry out, groan, show pain. Nor did he seem to notice being rescued. He showed nothing but patience.

Buckling himself into his seat, Fletch said, "He seems to accept all this."

The hyenas surrounded the airplane.

Carr said, "He knows he done wrong."

"Strip and dip," Carr said.

Fletch already had his sneakers and wool socks off. Carr had said he did not want to guess the temperature in either degrees centigrade or Fahrenheit. He said figuring such an astronomical number would thin his hair.

It was hot.

The other side of the none-too-serious fence, behind the fishing lodge's cabins, were a few of the Turkana tribe. Not all wore clothes.

Fletch dropped his cutoff ski pants. He plunged into the swimming pool.

"YOW!"

Standing on the pool edge, Carr laughed. "Something to write home about?"

"This is impossible! It's freezing! Is it just the contrast, because I'm so hot?"

"No. The water temperature really is near freezing."

Fletch's teeth were chattering. "How do they do it?"

The fishing lodge at Lake Turkana was a terrace, an open wooden lodge, and a half-dozen wooden cabins on a sand bluff overlooking the lake.

"They don't do it. The rate of evaporation in this heat is so rapid the water in a pool like this gets very cold indeed. Would you believe it?"

Hugging his own shoulders, Fletch said, "I believe it. You coming in?"

"Not on your life. You think I'm crazy?"

Fletch did a fast crawl to the ladder and pulled himself out of the pool.

"Swimming pools are for tourists," Carr said.

"This one sure is."

Fletch stood shivering on the pool ledge. Carr looked down Fletch's body and frowned. "Is that a birthmark?"

Fletch looked down at himself. The lowest right side of his stomach was blue. The mark was bigger than a fist. It was as big as an outstretched hand.

Fletch said, "I must have been born again."

Carr leaned over and prodded Fletch's flesh with his fingers. "First birthmark I ever saw that's swollen."

"I didn't even feel it," Fletch said. "I must have bumped into something in the hotel room. A strange hotel room. In the dark . . ."

"Sorry," Carr said. "None of my business."

Fletch prodded with his own fingers the great blue welt where Barbara had hit him. It didn't hurt.

Carr said, "I'll be on the terrace, when you're ready. I'll buy us shandies before lunch."

For a moment, Fletch sat on the pool edge, his feet in the cold water.

Then he dropped forward into the water. He thought of drowning.

Shortly he climbed out of the pool. He pulled on his cutoff ski pants, his socks, laced his sneakers, and went to join Carr on the terrace.

Fletch sat with Carr at the little table on the terrace on the sand bluff overlooking Lake Turkana. "A lake in the middle of a desert," Fletch said.

Carr said, "The lake is down about a mile from its edges since I've known it."

In the airplane coming in, Fletch had watched the Kerio River wandering over sand toward Lake Turkana. The river dried up miles before it reached the lake. A sad, empty landscape surrounded the lake, miles and miles in every direction. The only marks upon the landscape, besides the few, widely separated shambas, were water catchments, which were empty.

"The lake of many names." Carr gazed over it. "Aman, Galana, Basso Narok, Jade Sea, Lake Rudolf, Lake Turkana. There are Nile River perch in it. Explain that to me. They used to grow to as much as two hundred pounds. Nowadays, they run thirty, forty pounds."

Naked men on logs were fishing the lake.

A waiter brought two glasses, two bottles of premium beer, two bottles of lemon carbonated drink. "Thank you, Fred," Carr said. He poured some of the beer and some of the lemon drink in each glass to make the shandies.

"Over there is Koobi Fora." Carr tipped his head to the east side of the lake as he poured. "Where they found the remains of extinct elephants, both African and Indian. Explain to me how the skeletons of Indian elephants come to be here. Also seven human footprints, dated a million and a half years old. And, although some debate it, the remains of our first human ancestor, *Homo erectus*. First man. The papa of us all."

To the eye, the other side of the lake was just rolling sand. Fletch said, "Lots to be explained."

"I'll say."

A small, naked boy with a tall stack of aluminum pots on his head was trudging straight-backed through the sand from the village behind the lodge toward the lake.

"One can't imagine what the landscape might have been like here when it first cradled human life," Carr said. "Sure makes one curious."

Fletch tried his shandy. "Is the research why McCoy flew here?" Then he took a thirst-quenching drink.

"I don't know." Carr blinked. "I didn't ask him. Science wallah named Richard Leakey is in charge of all."

"I can see why you're digging around, looking for a lost Roman city."

"What I'm doing is nothing. I'm just trying to go back a few thousand years." From the terrace, Carr was scanning the horizon. "The landscape sort of calls for it. Here, in East Africa, you have sort of a time capsule, or time map. All of animate life before our very eyes, much of it still walking around, the rest being ghosts calling to us to be discovered. Here we all want to read the bones."

Using only their hands as paddles, the fishermen straddling logs were coming in toward shore.

Fletch took another long swallow. "Carr, I was sort of surprised when you left our wounded man at the police station."

Flying in, Carr had buzzed the lodge in the plane, signaling the manager, Hassan, to send a car for them. He had not been able to get the lodge on the radio.

While they were waiting at the airstrip, a man looking more ancient than Fletch had ever seen, longevity walking briskly in a loincloth, carrying a spear, marched out from under a bush. Carr said this man would be in charge of the airplane while they were at the fishing lodge.

"I've never seen anyone so old," Fletch said. "How old is he?"

"Right," Carr said. "About my age." Fletch figured Carr to be in his late forties.

The Land-Rover which brought them to the village was driven so fast over the packed sand road Fletch was sure it would fall apart. He was sure the man's split skull would fall apart.

"Did you see a hospital?" Carr upended his glass. "The colonists were better at building police stations than hospitals."

They had left the wounded man propped on a wooden bench inside the police station. Carr had explained everything to the only officer there. When they left, the police officer was still working on papers at his school-sized desk. He had only glanced at the wounded man when Carr had said he was a thief.

And the wounded man had watched them leave with eyes of weary patience.

"What will they do with him?" Fletch asked.

"I don't know. Maybe put him back in the bush. Or into the lake." Crossing Ferguson Gulf to the lodge in an aluminum outboard boat, they went through a herd of crocodiles. Flamingos stood in the shallower water. "McCoy is right, you know. One shouldn't meddle too much. I was indulging my own conscience."

"You were being kind."

"Kind to myself. That's the hell of original sin, you see. One can never be quite sure what is kindness to another."

Near the water's edge, the little boy with the pots on his head was doing a crazy dance in the sand. None of the pots fell off his head.

Watching Fletch watching the boy, Carr said, "Once in a small village way out in the bush, I saw a woman buy a postage stamp. She put the postage stamp on her head face-down, and then placed a rock on the stamp, to walk home that way. Made great sense. That way the glue on the stamp wouldn't get sweated away, and the stamp wouldn't blow away."

"I doubt I could walk two meters with a rock on my head," Fletch said. "Or a postage stamp."

Carr said, "My witch friend in Thika says you're carrying a whole box of rocks."

Fletch said nothing.

One of the fishermen who had emerged from the lake, shoving his log ashore, grabbed up the small boy. Holding the boy to his chest, the man danced in circles. The pots flew off the boy's head and scattered everywhere in the sand.

"Instead of wondering what the land tells us," Carr said, "right now, I'm wondering what the sky is trying to tell us. I think we'd better eat."

"Okay." Finishing his drink, moving slowly in the heat, Fletch watched the naked man and boy give the pots a quick rinse in the lake.

Entering the lodge's dining porch, Fletch saw the man and boy, hand in hand, begin their trudge through the sand back toward the village. Again, all the pots were stacked tall on the kid's head.

"What's that? What's happening?"

Facing the inside wall of the dining porch, Fletch looked to his left. The screens were bending toward him. Paper plates were three meters in the air. An empty beer bottle smashed on the stone floor.

Suddenly the air had darkened, yellowed.

"Eat fast!" Carr shouted over the roar. He cupped one hand over his plate. His other hand shoveled food into his mouth rapidly.

"What is it?" Fletch's eyes were stinging. He could barely see the great lumps of white fish yellowing on his plate.

"Sandstorm! My timing was off. The faster you eat now, the less of a peck of dirt you'll eat all at once."

Fletch put fish into his mouth. He coughed. Already his mouth was full of sand. Already a million particles of sand had adhered to the insides of his nostrils.

His filled plate wobbled on the table.

He and Carr both shoved back as the table was pulled up by the wind. It flipped over and skittered to the wall of the porch.

Carr and Fletch sat facing each other, hands in their laps, no table between them.

Fletch shouted, "Shall we go someplace else for dessert?"

Carr stood up. "I'll ask Hassan to get a cabin ready for us. The only thing for us to do in a sandstorm is get between walls and underneath a sheet."

As soon as Fletch stood up, his chair fell over. All the porch furniture was sliding by them. "How long does a sandstorm last?"

"A few hours. A day. A week."

"Can I call Barbara? Tell her we'll be late?"

"Sure," Carr said. "There's a telephone box at the corner. Right next to the pizza parlor!"

+++++++++++++++

"Carr? I saw a murder."

They were in narrow beds in a small cabin. It had grown dark.

The wind howled. Sand blew through the walls. Lying under the sheet, Fletch had kept his mouth closed. Still, his tongue, teeth were gritty with sand. Occasionally, he had spat into a glass. Carr suggested he stop that, saying his body needed the fluid. Fletch kept his eyes closed until his lips became too heavy with sand. Then he'd roll over and wipe his face against the lower sheet. The sheets became coated with sand centimeters thick. Less than every hour, he would get up and flip the sand off his sheets. Sand was in his eyes, nose, mouth, sinuses, in his skin. He wished he could keep his nostrils closed.

There was a primitive shower in the cabin. It dripped in loud splats. When Fletch could hear the shower splattering he knew the wind was down somewhat. Mostly he couldn't hear the shower.

At the moment, he could hear the shower splattering.

Carr asked, "Is that the box of rocks you're carrying?"

"I guess so."

Carr said, "I've got strong legs, too."

The cabin was hit with another sustained blast of hot, sand-filled wind.

"At the airport yesterday," Fletch said when he was hearing the shower splattering again. "Just after we arrived." Talking, he realized just how much sand was in his throat, mouth, on his lips.

"I went into the men's room while Barbara changed some money. There was a man in there, acting perfectly normal, just washing up. I went into a cabinet. Another man came in. I saw his feet. The two men argued. They were shouting in a language I didn't understand. Maybe Portuguese. When I came out, there was only one man there, and he was dead. Stabbed. Blood all over the place."

"The same man who was there when you entered?"

"No. The other man."

"So you saw the murderer."

"Yes."

"What did you do?"

"Carr, I threw up. I was careful to wipe my fingerprints off the door as I left."

"Could you identify the murderer?"

"Yes. I saw him again, in the parking lot, as we were driving away."

"A white man?"

"Yes. They were both white."

"I saw about it in *The Nation*."

"I forgot to look in the newspapers."

"Murders still make headlines here. Unless it's just Dan Dawes doing his nocturnal duty."

"It wasn't Dan Dawes."

"No. That's not how Dan executes people. Whom have you told?"

"Only Barbara. Now you."

"I see. You made your decision to shut up about this pretty fast."

"What do you mean?"

"You wiped your fingerprints off the door handle."

"Carr, I had just arrived in a foreign country. I knew very little about Kenya."

"There is justice here."

"A murder investigation is apt to take a long time."

"Right."

"Soon, I've got to go home, back to work, start my married life. You know?"

"Of course."

An extraordinary wall of wind slammed against the cabin. Fletch said, "Committed, but not involved."

After that thick wall of wind passed, Fletch said, "Did the newspapers say who the murdered man was?"

"I didn't really read it. Did you recognize either man from your airplane?"

Fletch thought a moment. "I don't know. The airplane was so crowded."

"Well," Carr said, "it seems to me you made your decision. You were a witness to a murder, and you chose not to come forward."

"Yeah, but, Carr? Suppose they convict the wrong guy?"

"There's always that possibility. They'll hang him. You'll never know. You'll be in the United States downing hot dogs and beer."

"I don't want to live with that possibility."

After a while, Carr said, "That's a box of rocks, all right. You can't wait around Kenya for a year or more serving as police witness. And you have a natural disinclination against letting the powers-that-be hang the wrong chap."

Carr didn't say any more.

++++++++++++++

"Carr?" It was hours later, but Fletch knew Carr wasn't asleep. Shortly before there had been another loud burst of wind. Now the splattering shower could be heard again. "Tell me about my father."

"What? Sorry. My ears aren't that perfect, you know."

"My father. Tell me about him."

"We're talking about the man Fletcher."

"Please."

"Well. He's a pilot. Like the rest of us, he's flown light planes here and there in the world. Somewhere in South America for a while, and then I know he flew in India. He was well off, for a while. He owned three airplanes, his own little airlines, in Ethiopia. Then that new administration took over, and took over his airlines."

"Just took them over?"

"Yes."

"Didn't pay him for them, or anything?"

"Because they wanted his airplanes, they also took over his house and his car, to get rid of him. Everything. That government enterprises freely only on its own behalf."

"Oh."

"So he arrived in Kenya broke. Flew for me for a while. Now he has his own airplane again."

"You have more than one airplane?"

"I have two."

The wind made conversation impossible for a few moments.

"Carr?" Fletch finally asked. "Is he a happy man? Does he give the impression life satisfies him?"

"Pretty much. Flying around is a great life. Aren't you having fun?"

+++++++++++++++

"Carr?" It was the time of night any dawn would seem a wearisome blessing. The wind was down for the moment, but Fletch knew it would rise again. He felt like a stocking stuffed with sand. "We didn't anchor down the airplane. What's to keep it from flipping over?"

"Remember that little guy at the airstrip you thought was so old?"

"Yeah."

"He's out there in the wind, hanging on to a wing holding the airplane down."

"You serious?"

"Of course I'm serious."

"That skinny little old guy will get blown away, too."

"We'll see."

"So you two finally decided to show up?"

Barbara was in a long chair by the swimming pool at the Norfolk Hotel.

"What?" Carr said.

"What?" Fletch said.

Even the sky over Nairobi still wasn't that clear.

"Safe and sound." Carr rubbed his hands together. "But not home on the same day. Anyone else want a beer?"

Fletch stooped to kiss Barbara.

"You look all puffy," Barbara said.

"What?"

"Puffy!"

"We're full of sand."

"Don't shout."

Fletch sneezed.

"I want a beer." Carr signaled the pool *bwana* on the upper terrace.

"Were you guys up all night?" Barbara asked. "Your eyes are runny."

"She wants to know if we spent the night drinking and dancing."

"Yes," Carr said. "We spent the night drinking and dancing."

On the other side of the pool were an English couple in string bikinis and straw hats under an umbrella having a proper tea.

"We were in a sandstorm," Fletch said.

"Sure."

"We were in a sandstorm."

"I hear you."

"Not that bad a time." Carr sat in a poolside chair. "I don't mind sand." He was speaking as does a person who can't hear himself. "Your husband saw the cradle of humanity." He sneezed. "Perhaps where man first walked."

"Sure."

Fletch sat on the edge of Barbara's long chair. "This little old guy, he couldn't weigh sixty pounds, held the wing of the plane down all night, so it wouldn't flip in the wind."

"Why are you two talking so loudly?"

"What?" Carr asked. He now had beer in hand.

"My, you're gritty." Barbara's hand was on Fletch's forearm. "Don't they have water in whatever lake you were at?"

"Crocodiles, too."

"Sure."

Fletch's tongue continuously ran over the sand on his teeth.

Carr said, "Life's not all roasted goat."

Barbara said, "I hope not."

"What?" Fletch asked.

"I'll admit it wasn't a very good flight home." Carr shook his head. "Couldn't see."

"You were supposed to be back in time for dinner last night."

"There was a sandstorm, you see," Fletch said.

"I had some fruit in my room."

"Oh?" Carr said. "Did he leave politely?"

"Why didn't you call?"

"Wives always want to know why you don't call home," Carr said. "That's the way it is with wives."

"There were no phones, Barbara."

"A fishing lodge without phones?"

"The madame wouldn't let us," Carr said. "She said the brothel's phones were for paying customers only."

"Did it ever cross your mind I might be worried?"

"We were almost sanded down a full size." Fletch sneezed.

"Did you catch cold?"

"Air-conditioned brothel," Carr said.

"Sand." Fletch sneezed. "Sinuses." He sneezed again. "Oh, hell."

"Hope that's all you caught."

"Didn't go fishing." Fletch sneezed. The English couple looked over at him with concern. "Nile perch there. Crocodiles in the lake and the fishermen go out on it straddling logs, their legs and feet in the water."

"What was I supposed to do if you didn't show up?"

"We did show up." Carr sneezed.

"Any word from my father?"

"No."

Fletch stood up. "I've got to take a shower. Start getting this sand off. Thanks for a lovely trip." Fletch sneezed. "Carr."

+++++++++++++

Barbara came into the bathroom as Fletch was getting out of the shower. He had rinsed his mouth and nose and eyes, washed his hair, and scrubbed his body over and over again. He still felt like the inside of a cement mixer.

"I was worried," Barbara said. "Worried sick."

"There were no phones, Barbara. No radio that could work."

"All day yesterday I sat here feeling sorry for the way I acted yesterday morning. For the things I said. Then you didn't show up. Didn't call. All night."

"We were in a sandstorm near the Ethiopian border. There were no camels coming this way."

"Then I began to get angry all over again. Angry and scared."

Fletch banged the side of his head with the heel of his hand. "If my ears don't pop soon, I'm going to go nuts. I feel like I've got a balloon in my head."

"Then you two come prancing in this afternoon looking like a couple of kids who had been playing in the sandbox."

"We flew home at twelve thousand five hundred feet," Fletch said, "with the window open. Otherwise, Carr couldn't see. The sandstorm reached that high. Even the cockpit was full of sand. Can you understand all that? We're deaf. Our ears hurt. Carr kept having to open the window."

"Did you stay away all night because of the way I acted yesterday morning? Were you trying to teach me a lesson or something?"

"Oh Jesus, Barbara. If I ever play that sort of game on you, I'll let you know. Where are my swimming trunks?"

Fletch went into the bedroom.

"In the top drawer of the bureau."

"Good thing we knew there was a swimming pool at the ski lodge. At least we have swimsuits."

The two pairs of skis stood in a corner of the room. The other side of the window next to them, hibiscus flowered.

"What was I supposed to think when you didn't show up?"

"That we were caught in a sandstorm near the Ethiopian border. Maybe a swim will help blow the sand out of my sinuses."

"What's that?" Wide-eyed, Barbara was staring at Fletch's lower stomach.

"What do you think?"

"I don't know. What is it?"

"A wound, Barbara. A trauma. Vulgarly described as a blow below the belt."

"Where did you get it?"

"Are you serious?"

"Of course I'm serious. Where did that come from?"

"You belted me."

"I did not."

"No one else did. Ever."

"Not like that."

"Like that."

"I never did."

"Oh, stow it. You coming back to the pool for a swim?"

"I'll take a shower."

"Okay. I'll go for a swim. Then play in the sandbox for a while." Fletch sneezed. "When I come back, we can think about what we do next."

"If you don't make it," Barbara said, "telephone."

"So," Barbara said.

"So," Fletch said.

They had ordered breakfast on the Lord Delamere Terrace.

"Here we are in Nairobi."

"So we are."

"Having a honeymoon at last."

"And a night's sleep." Across Harry Thuku Road, Nairobi University was awake with students coming and going in the bright sunlight.

"A nice, long night. Ten hours to sleep, and five hours to eat and play."

"That much?"

"By my clock."

"I feel like a new man." Fletch began to look through *The Standard*. "Except my ears are still clogged and my nose is still runny."

"This morning I'm glad I married you." Under the table, Barbara's leg went against his.

"Likewise."

"I was afraid that thing on your stomach would hurt."

"It doesn't. It never did. Just looks ugly."

"I don't know. I think it looks sort of erotic."

"One is apt to think well of one's own work."

"I didn't do that to you."

"Oh."

"I know I didn't. You must have bumped into something."

"Okay."

"It looks sort of like a codpiece pulled aside. A jockstrap or something, you know?"

"Maybe you ought to go into the business of Designer Bruises."

"Is that why hitting boxers below the belt is considered a no-no?"

"Their trainers haven't your sense of what's sexy, I guess."

"I didn't know men are so sensitive there."

"If you cut us, do we not bleed?"

Their fruit was served.

"There's nothing in this morning's newspaper about the murder at the airport," Fletch said after the waiter left.

"Did you tell Carr about it?"

"Yes." The mashed rhubarb was sweetened exactly right.

"What did he say about it?"

"He agrees I have a problem. A 'box of rocks.' "

"Did he understand why you didn't come forward?"

"Oh, yes. I can't spend my life in Kenya reviewing their suspects, one by one."

"Are you just going to forget about the murder?"

"I can't. Suppose they decide to hang the wrong sack?"

"Can't you just leave a description with the police?"

"Oh, yeah, sure. Middle-aged white man with brown hair and a moustache. Kenya probably has more men fitting that description than they have zebras. They'd have me flying halfway around the world and back again every week. Which I can't afford. Which Kenya probably can't afford. So I suspect they'd ask me to stay here, in voices sweet or stern. Which I also can't afford. Carr had no suggestions."

"Speaking of *afford* . . ." Barbara cleared her throat.

"I've already thought of it."

"Your father doesn't seem to be Nairobi's greeter, official or unofficial. This is the third day we've been here, and no Fletcher senior has showed up pulling a welcome wagon."

"I've noticed. There was a message from him, however. While we were out at Thika."

"Yes. Saying he'd be back."

"He must have had a flat tire."

"I think you'd better check with the hotel desk, to make sure our bills are being paid."

"I thought we'd have breakfast first."

"I doubt we'll get much of our money back from the ski lodge in Colorado. We don't deserve much back."

"They must be used to canceled honeymoons."

All sorts of interesting traffic was going by on Harry Thuku Road. Besides the cars, taxis, trucks usual to any city, there were *safari guarris* painted in zebra stripes, Land-Rovers with spare wheels plastered all over their bodies, Jeeps which looked like they had been rolled down mountains sideways and a few vehicles which looked distinctly homemade.

"So what will we do today?" Barbara asked. "Presuming we don't have to find a cheaper hotel."

Their eggs, bacon, and toast were served.

"I suppose I could go looking for my father. He must be here, somewhere. I am 'mildly curious.' "

"A lady at the pool yesterday told me about seeing some wonderful dancers, what did she call them? Bomas. The Bomas Harambee Dancers. Something like that. About ten kilometers from here. She said they tell this wonderful story in dance about an evil spirit who takes over a young girl while she and her husband are traveling, asleep in the bush. So the young husband goes and hires a witch doctor to rid his wife of the evil spirit. The doctor comes and traces the evil spirit away from the girl. But every time he gets close to the spirit, the spirit scares the followers of the witch doctor and runs away. The whole story is told in dance. I might like to see that this afternoon."

Fletch was watching Juma striding down the street toward them.

"And would you believe there's a game park just outside Nairobi that's something like forty-seven square miles? Lions, giraffes, everything. We could rent a car, if you don't mind driving on the left side of the road."

Striding along, shirtless, shoeless in dusty shorts, carrying a book in his left hand, Juma kept his happy eyes straight ahead. He did not survey the people on Lord Delamere's Terrace.

Fletch and Barbara were too far back in the terrace to call out to him.

"Someone else said there's a great restaurant called the Tamarind. Great lobster. And a Chinese restaurant near here, called the Hong Kong. Less expensive. Best soup in the world."

"You've been doing your homework."

Fletch was just getting up to go after Juma, to say hello to him, when he saw Juma turn into the entrance of the Norfolk Hotel.

Putting the book in his back pocket, Juma bounced through the tables and chairs at them.

He sat down at their table.

"Are you happy to see me?" he asked.

"Absolutely," Fletch answered.

"Does that mean yes?"

"Of course. Were you looking for us?"

Juma's eyebrows wrinkled.

"Have you spent all this time in Nairobi?" Barbara asked.

"Yes."

"Would you like something to eat?" Barbara asked.

"I will have some toast," Juma said, "to be polite." Barbara handed him her plate of toast. "Also because I like buttered toast."

"What have you been doing?" Fletch asked, attempting to make conversation.

"I've been thinking about your problem, Fletch."

"What problem?"

"You see, my father is in jail, too."

Barbara jumped.

"Very sad, very stupid." Juma munched his toast. "You see, he was a driver for the government. The department of education. At the end of an eleven-hour day, very tired and hungry, he went into this bar where his brother works, for some food. Someone reported seeing this government car parked outside this bar for forty-five minutes. For this, he was convicted and sentenced to jail for eighteen months."

"Good God," Barbara said.

Fletch felt the blood draining from his face. "Good God."

"It is not proper for a government car to be seen parked outside a bar."

"Eighteen months in jail?" Fletch asked.

Barbara was staring at Fletch.

"Also, he was fired. So my family has no money again. May I have more toast, please?" Juma took another slice.

Fletch cleared his throat. "Who said my father is in jail?"

"It is something you will have to accept, Fletch. I know you came all this way from America to see him. Have you seen him?"

Fletch felt a throbbing in his temples. "No."

"That's the problem," Juma said. "They won't let me see my father, either. Even now."

"How do you know my father is in jail?"

"This man at the jail, the one who keeps me out, no matter what I say, says not permitting my father to see his son all this long time is part of the punishment, you see. For parking the government car outside the bar."

Barbara said, "Poor Fletch."

"So I asked this man if he would make an exception for you, because you came all this way to see your father, and he said, maybe, but not until after the trial."

Fletch sat back in his chair. He exhaled deeply.

Barbara said, "Oh, dear."

Juma asked Barbara, "How do you like Kenya?"

"Just great," Fletch answered.

"We *wananchi* are very proud of Kenya. Everything is very scrupulous here. Do you see pictures of our president, Daniel arap Moi, just everywhere?"

"Just everywhere," Barbara answered. "In every shop."

"Although I admit it is difficult on a family when a father is sentenced to eighteen months in jail for parking a government car outside a bar."

"I daresay," Fletch said.

"So I have been thinking about your problem, Fletch." Juma shrugged. "I do not have a solution."

Barbara was still staring at Fletch. "Have you known about this?"

"Not really."

"What do you mean, *not really*?"

"Not now, Barbara. Please. Not here." Fletch felt he was being wrung out to dry.

"You did know about this. *Flat tire*, you said."

"I didn't."

"Why is he in jail?"

"It must have happened yesterday."

"There was some trouble at the Thorn Tree," Juma said. "Everyone knew about it."

"I didn't," Barbara said. "What's the Thorn Tree?"

So filled was Fletch's head and heart that he did not realize Carr was standing over them until Carr spoke.

"Irwin, I need a quiet word with you."

"Ah. Good morning, Carr."

"We've heard," Barbara said.

Carr looked at her. "You've heard what?"

"Fletch's father is in jail. Awaiting trial. No visitors."

"I see." Sitting down, Carr nodded hello at Juma. "He turned himself in yesterday. By far the wiser course."

"Has he got a lawyer?" Fletch asked.

"Yes."

Barbara asked, "What's all this about?"

"Two nights ago," Carr told her, "while we were eating at the Shade Hotel, there was some sort of a punch-up at the Thorn Tree Café. Such things didn't used to be unusual, in the bad old days. Walter Fletcher may, or may not, have started it. Damage to the glassware was done. Much worse, in the eyes of the authorities, a few tourists were discommoded. Walter Fletcher may, or may not, have knocked an *askari* silly."

"What's an *askari*?" Barbara asked.

"A guard. The official status of this particular guard is not yet established."

"You mean, there's still some doubt as to whether he was a cop or a private watchman?" Fletch asked.

"Yes," answered Carr. "Some private guards have police status. Some don't. May I have some coffee?" Carr asked the waiter. "It makes a difference. Kenya is very strict about respect for its things and people official."

"Eighteen months for parking a government car in front of a bar," Fletch muttered. "It's a wonder they didn't send Dan Dawes to shoot Juma's father!"

"Why can't they find out?" Barbara asked.

"Because the *askari* is still moaning it up in the hospital, claiming this and that between bites of noodles. He says one of his wives has his employment papers, but he can't remember which one."

"Which *wife*?" Barbara asked.

"I guess a clip on the jaw causes one to forget which wife is which." Carr sipped his hot coffee. "In any case, no one can see Walter Fletcher, except his lawyer, until after the trial. And the trial date is not set."

Juma said, "It will be nice to get away from here."

Carr gave him a sharp look.

"What can we do for him?" Fletch asked.

"There's a mosque down the street." Carr sipped more of his coffee. "Be sure and take off your shoes. There's a sign on the main gate saying, *Do Not Encourage Beggars*."

"Oh, dear," Barbara said. "Poor Fletch."

"We shouldn't have gone to Thika with you," Fletch said. "Because my father didn't show up when he was supposed to, I acted snotty. I wasn't here when he did show up."

"Water over the dam," Carr said.

"Well, there isn't that much water in Africa," Fletch said.

"Walter's over the dam," Barbara said.

"Which brings up the next point," Carr said.

"There's nothing I can do for him?" Fletch asked.

"No."

"I can't see him?"

"No."

"Shit!"

"Today I'm flying down to my digs," Carr said. "Get some work done on them. I thought I'd stop by first, bring you up to date on affairs Walter Fletcher, and ask if you'd like to come with me."

"To your digs?" Fletch asked.

"Oh," Barbara said. "Now we go looking for a lost Roman city."

"It's not a very grand camp. You'll be living under canvas. And it's hot there." Carr looked at the wall of the Norfolk Hotel. "But it would be cheaper for you than staying at this palace of eternal delights. And it might be interesting for you. See something of the real Kenya."

Fletch sighed. He looked at Barbara.

"Bomas Harambee," Barbara said.

"What?" Carr said. "That's right. Let's pull together for our own sakes. You might even help me root through the jungle. No telling what we might find."

Fletch, too, looked at the wall of the hotel. "Barbara? I want you to be precisely clear as to what you want to do."

Barbara sat up in her chair. She swallowed. Carr, Juma, and Fletch were watching her. She swallowed again. "How can I agree to something when I don't know what I'm agreeing to?"

"Rather nasty living," Carr said. "In tents, at the edge of the jungle. No telephones, electricity, or ice cream parlors. What we're doing is hacking our way through the jungle, either side of a river. Digging holes, here and there, seeing if they turn up anything vaguely ancient Roman. Still, Sheila likes it."

Barbara was staring at Fletch.

"Barbara?" Fletch asked. "Would you like to go home?"

"It is our honeymoon," she said.

"One of the all-time great ones," Fletch said.

"Sheila could use a bit of company," Carr said.

"I don't see how we can go home," Barbara said. "We came all this way to meet your father."

"True," Fletch said. "But his absence here is just as real as his absence is in the States."

"But now you know he exists," Barbara said.

"True."

"And probably you'll never be able to come back."

"Probably not."

"And there is this other matter . . ." Barbara looked at Carr. ". . . no one knows what to do about."

Carr said nothing.

Barbara said, "Why are you leaving it to me?"

Fletch sighed.

"Is it something you want to do?" Barbara asked.

"I don't know any more than you do."

"Nice time," Juma said.

Everyone looked at Juma.

Carr then looked at his watch. "It's getting nigh onto checkout time. If you're checking out, that is."

Barbara said, "Okay."

Fletch said to Carr, "I'm afraid we're not being very gracious about your kind invitation."

Carr grinned. "Didn't I show you a nice time at Lake Turkana?"

25

"I'm not sure just what arrangements have been made."
Fletch, in speaking to the man in the hotel's cashier cage,
hesitated. "The name is Fletcher." The sound of his own
name made him slightly sick. The pin on the cashier's coat
said his name was Lincoln. "We wish to check out this
morning. We don't know if we're coming back to the Norfolk. We hope to."

The cashier pulled a long card from a file box. "Yes,
Mr. Fletcher." He looked at the card. "Your expenses are
being paid. By Walter Fletcher. No problem."

"If we go and come back again will our expenses still
be paid?"

"Unless Walter Fletcher directs otherwise, we'll leave
the bill open. You just sign for your expenses so far, and
we'll free the room." He turned the card around and slid it
under the grille to Fletch with a pen. "Going on safari?"

"Yes." Fletch signed the bill, which was in *shillingi*.
"We're going on safari. We weren't invited until just now.
Also, there'll be a breakfast charge coming in from the ter-
race."

"Are you going to Masai Mara?"

"I'm not sure where we're going. Someplace south. Near
a river."

"You should go to Masai Mara," the cashier said. "It's
nice there."

Fletch slid the billing card and pen back under the grille.
"And I want to thank the hotel for the new sneakers."

The cashier smiled. "Nice time."

++++++++++++++

"Good grief." In their room, Barbara was stuffing ski
suits, mittens, earmuffs, thermal underwear, and woolen
socks into the big, framed knapsacks. "If you'd told me a
week ago we'd be heading off today to search for a lost
Roman city on the East African coast today, I wouldn't
think you were crazy, I'd know it!"

"I wouldn't be so crazy as to predict such a thing."

"Do you think there's anything to it? Is there any chance
of our finding such a place? I mean, my God, Carr's best
source of information seems to be a witch doctor!"

Fletch shrugged. "It's Carr's thing. It's what he wants
to do. He's inviting us into his life. I appreciate it."

"Daft," Barbara said. "How could the Romans have
built a city here in East Africa without its being a known,
established, historical fact by now?"

"I don't think very much of history is known," Fletch
said. "Percentage wise, I mean. Look how hard it is to find
out the facts of my own, personal history."

"Going into the African jungle to dig holes," Barbara
said. "Are we sure we want to do this?"

"I just got a look at our hotel bill," Fletch said. "It's in
shillingi, of course, but many thousands of *shillingi*. Carr

says my father is not rich. I don't think we should stay here racking up such a bill, if we have a choice. Carr has given us a choice."

"Your blue jeans and T-shirt are back from the laundry. They're hanging in the closet."

"Great. I can dress like a bum again, instead of a street-walker."

"Fletch, are you sure you and Carr aren't related?"

Hanger in hand, Fletch was looking at his jeans. "You mean, is Carr my father?"

"At the pool last night, when you came back from Lake Turkana, I don't know, watching you enter, the way you both walked, the way you sat, the way you both spoke . . ."

"We had both just been sandblasted, kept awake all night by a raging storm, deafened in the airplane . . . 'course we moved and sounded alike."

"He's being awfully nice to us."

"My jeans have been pressed. Look! My jeans have been pressed!"

"Oh, dear. That won't do." She took the jeans from him and started to rough them up in her hands.

"I've thought about this," he said. "Want the hard evidence?"

"About what?"

"While we were out at Thika and Karen with Carr, someone came to the hotel, identified himself as Walter Fletcher, and inquired for us."

"Couldn't do that by phone?"

"The man at the reception desk said that someone came to the hotel. He said it was Walter Fletcher." Barbara was kicking his jeans around the floor. "When we met Juma, he said he knows my father."

"He sounded regretful about Walter Fletcher, too."

"Juma identified Walter Fletcher as a pilot. Carr was with us. Juma knows Carr, and he knows a man here named

Fletcher. When he came to the hotel this morning, before Carr, he knew Walter Fletcher is in jail."

"My father-in-law the jailbird."

"Please, Barbara."

"Well, it's true, isn't it?"

"Is hitting below the belt a characteristic of yours?"

"A man who starts a fight in a bar! And gets arrested for it! Mother will love that one. I married the son of a jailbird!"

"God damn it, Barbara!" Fletch snatched his jeans off the floor. "Is this what marriage to you is? You're nice to me in public and vicious in private. Downstairs, on the terrace, you were full of *Oh, dear! Poor Fletch!* and up here you call me the son of a jailbird!"

"Well, I've had time to think."

"I'm not in control of the facts, here, regarding my own life." Fletch was falling over trying to get into his jeans. "Sorry. We just have to go along discovering what we can discover."

"You said, 'Maybe he got a flat tire.' Really, Fletch. Yesterday, Carr said your father was delayed by some 'legal difficulty.' You call those *facts*?"

Fletch zipped his jeans. "I knew there'd been some unpleasantness in a café. I didn't know he was in jail. Clearly, I didn't know that."

Barbara said, "I don't want any of this to be true!"

"At least he turned himself in."

"Why wouldn't it have been natural for your father to meet us at the airport?"

"I don't know."

"He didn't do it."

"I guess he didn't."

Fletch was pulling on his T-shirt.

"You 'guess'? What is this with you and the word *guess*? When you married me, you didn't say *I do*, you said, *I guess I do*."

"I guess I did." Sitting on the edge of the bed, Fletch was pulling on his socks and sneakers.

"What do you mean, you *guess* your father wasn't at the airport to meet us? You know damn right well he wasn't."

"Do I?" Fletch headed for the door.

"Where are you going?"

"That's the point, Barbara. I don't."

"Are you going somewhere?"

"Yes." He opened the door to the corridor.

"Where?"

"Out."

"Carr's waiting for us."

"He said he'll pick us up at noon."

"You're disappearing again because you're mad at me."

"I'm going out . . ." Hand still on the door handle, Fletch hesitated. ". . . to answer your question; to find out something for myself: maybe to find out too much."

"Fletch . . ."

"If I'm not back by the time Carr gets here, you'll just have to wait for me."

"Hello." Fletch waited for the young policeman behind the high counter to look up, notice him, answer him.

"Hello," the policeman answered after only a glance.

Fletch sneezed. "How are you?"

"Well, thank you. And yourself?"

"I'm fine."

The policeman glanced at Fletch again. "What do you want at a police station?"

Fletch swallowed. "I want to see my father. My name is Fletcher. Is he here?"

"Oh, yes." The policeman checked the second sheet of paper on a clipboard. "Awaiting trial."

"May I see him?"

"That's not the way it's supposed to be," the policeman said. "He is being punished, you see."

"He is being punished before his trial?"

The policeman's forehead creased. "What is the point of keeping him here if we let everyone see him?"

"I have come from America," Fletch said. "Arrived two days ago. I don't know how long I will be able to stay here. I have come to see him."

"Oh, I see." Moving around behind the counter, the policeman fiddled with papers. His brow remained creased.

Fletch said nothing more.

After a few moments, the policeman went through a door behind the counter.

Trying to clear his eyes and his nose and his throat of sand, Fletch had walked the half block from the Norfolk Hotel to the police station. The sidewalk was busy with people his age carrying books to and from Nairobi University. He passed an older, Caucasian couple in plaid shorts and straw hats looking exhausted and confused.

No one else was in the lobby of the police station. The place was absolutely quiet.

Fletch sneezed again.

The policeman returned alone.

He said nothing. Behind the counter, he started to sort some papers.

Fletch said, "Well? Any chance of my seeing him?"

"Mr. Fletcher is not in."

"What?"

"He says to tell you he is not in."

"Did you tell him I'm his son? His son is here to see him?"

"Oh, yes. He asked me to say he is not in."

Going toward the door to the street, Fletch sneezed.

Quietly, the policeman said, "Bless you."

Fletch turned around. "Walter Fletcher? Is the man you are holding named Walter Fletcher, originally an American, Caucasian, somewhere in his forties?"

"Oh, yes," the policeman said. "We know him well."

"Distract her hands," Carr muttered.

Fletch tickled the back of the little girl's neck.

As her hands flew up, Carr's huge, strong hands slipped the little girl's leg bone back into alignment. First she giggled; then she yelped.

"It's over, sweet. You'll be a beautiful dancer when you get older."

Carr slipped a strongly elastic brace over the girl's foot and up her leg. The cut over the compound fracture was almost healed. The leg had been broken a week or more. He then splinted the leg.

"We do what we can," Carr said. "Patent medicines."

They had flown southeast from Nairobi.

At Wilson Airport, Juma had helped carry things from the Land-Rover to the airplane, had helped pack them in, then climbed into the backseat beside Barbara. Fletch had heard nothing said by anyone about Juma's accompanying them. The snow skis were in the airplane's aisle, almost the full length of the plane.

On the flight, Juma read a book, *Ake*, by Wole Soyinka.

Chin in hand, Barbara studied the landscape through the window.

From the air, Carr's camp was barely noticeable. It was on the west side of the river in a natural clearing north of thick jungle. About twenty-five kilometers east sparkled the blue of the Indian Ocean.

The airstrip was just a two-wheeled track. There was a long cook tent, a small tent each side of it, and, at the front, a rectangular piece of canvas supported by four poles. A derelict Jeep was in the shade of a huge banyan tree.

Carr placed the airplane's wheels in the ground tracks precisely. Fletch pushed open the door beside him. The heat was immediate, intense, humid.

About fifty people moved slowly from under the trees to greet them.

Watching the people, Carr flipped off the switches on his instrument panel. "Clinic's open, I guess."

Monkeys were everywhere, on the ground, in the huge banyan tree, on top of the tents, on the table and chairs under the horizontal canvas. There were papa monkeys with baby monkeys on their backs; mamma monkeys with infant monkeys at their breasts; children monkeys playing their own games up and down and around, everywhere.

"They bite," Carr said. "They steal. They are no respecter of persons."

Sheila, in tennis shorts and a preppy shirt opened at the collar, waited for them at the end of the runway track. On the tray she carried was a pitcher of lemonade and glasses. "All's right here," Sheila sang out to Carr the minute he stepped out onto the wing. "All's right with you? Then all's right with the world."

"Find anything interesting while I was gone?" Carr asked.

"Yes," Sheila said. "The spare keys to the Land-Rover you insisted you lost."

Carr shrugged.

After putting the tray on the ground and pouring out the lemonade, Sheila hugged and kissed Carr. "My sweaty beast," she said. She hugged and kissed Fletch when she understood who he was. "Good. We need some more brawn." Hugged and kissed Barbara. "Excellent! A woman to catch me up with the world!"

Juma stood away, looking at Sheila sourly.

When Carr introduced them, Sheila gave a little wave of her hand. "Hello, there, Juma. Glad you came to join us."

"I actually brought some half-decent steaks," Carr said.

"I'm sure they were very dear."

"Not as dear as the chicken." A monkey was peering into the lemonade pitcher on the ground. Sheila gently guided it away with her boot.

Juma spoke quietly to Fletch. "Listen. Is that Carr's woman?"

"I guess so. Sheila. Yes."

Juma said, "I didn't know that."

"Nothing Roman turn up?" Carr asked Sheila as they walked toward the tents.

"Just the usual. Spear tips. A tusk. A skeleton."

"Human?"

"Yes. A child. Fairly recent, I think."

For much of the afternoon, in the shade of the extended cook tent, Fletch watched Carr doctor the people. Many children had burns, and Carr dressed them. Many, many others had eye infections, which Carr bathed. He put ointment into each infected eye and sent each mother or father away with a small tube and exact instructions. Other people had boils and sores and cuts and broken bones, complained of aching stomachs, and, in each case, Carr questioned, examined, reached into his kit for something that would clean, cure, fix, do no harm anyway. The people knew enough not even to ask him about their many spots of skin cancer. For two old men Carr thought had internal tumors he could do nothing and said so. He told them where he expected the Flying Doctor to be in a week or ten days.

A man who carried himself proudly limped in on a crude crutch made of a tree branch. He said he had dropped a rock and crushed his toes. Carr clipped off two toes with garden shears. He stitched, trimmed, disinfected, dressed them. A third toe, only broken, Carr set.

Carr wrapped the two severed toes in a piece of gauze and solemnly handed them to the man.

"How did these people know when you were coming?" Fletch asked Carr.

Carr didn't answer.

"How did Juma know all about my father? How did he know Barbara and I were having breakfast on the Lord Delamere Terrace at that moment? He came straight to us, without inquiring or appearing to look around. How did he seem to know we were coming down here before we did?"

Carr said, "Never try to figure out how Africans know things. It's their magic. But I can give you a clue. Much of their magic is simple observation. They spend what is to us an inordinate amount of time thinking about people. I mean real people, the people around them. They think about people instead of things, possessions, cars, televisions, hair dryers. They think about the people they know instead of thinking about mythical people, politicians, sports heroes, and movie stars; instead of thinking about mythical events, distant wars, currency crises, and meetings of the United Nations." Carr dropped an empty tube of Neosporin ointment into an oil drum being used as a wastebasket. "Our magic, of course, comes from the pharmacy. Out here we have a beautiful relationship, as long as we respect each other's magic."

"But why were they waiting for you?" Fletch was taking off his sneakers and wool socks. "Sheila could have treated their burns and infections . . ."

Carr opened a fresh roll of gauze. "They don't trust Sheila. If you didn't notice, Sheila is an Indian lady. She's tried to help, but they won't let her. Magic, everywhere, has to do with the *persona*. They also wouldn't trust you to help them, even though you are a white man. The older people would not be able to bring themselves to complain to you, to tell you they have problems, because you are too young. So I get these dirty jobs."

A young man explained to Carr that he'd had a sore on the back of his hand. So he had stuck his hand in battery acid. Now the hand, wrist, forearm were horribly inflamed.

As Fletch helped Carr, held this, held that, fetched a new box of medical supplies from the airplane, he watched a tent being set up in the clearing under Sheila's direction. His and Barbara's knapsacks were carried up from the plane and put into that tent.

Because the snow skis were so long, and so unusual, two men carried them to the tent on their shoulders. Fletch heard the exclamations as Barbara took the skis out of their cases and showed everyone what they were. Standing in the dirt in the tropical sun, the jungle a green wall behind her, Barbara went through the skiing motions with the ski poles, knees bent, hips sashaying, slaloming down a snow-sided mountain, from the looks of her.

Juma, in pretending to ski, pretended to lose his balance. On one leg, arms pinwheeling for a long time, he pretended to be trying to regain his balance. Finally, he let himself fall. Dust rose around him.

A large monkey, scolding angrily, tried to take one of the ski poles from Barbara.

After Carr treated the people, they wandered back into the jungle or the bush on narrow footpaths.

"Terrible eye troubles," Carr said. "So close to the equator, without protection from the sun. And there are always the flies." He waved a dozen flies away from a child's face. "And burns. The children try to help out with the cooking. They play too close to the fires. Or they fall out of their mother's breast-slings or back-slings into the fire. The mothers, you see: most of them are children themselves."

Most of the mothers were long-legged girls, skirted this way and that with *kangas*, wearing uncomfortably tight-looking metal bracelets and anklets, their breasts covered, if at all, with arrangements of necklaces. Whatever their troubles, all seemed in good spirits. They were attractively shy with Fletch, never looking directly at him, that he saw, but clearly talking about him, and Juma, and Barbara.

"Is this meddling?" Carr was getting tired. "I should ask the good Dr. McCoy if what we ordinary folks do here in the bush is meddling. What some of these bloody science chaps would like to do is put a glass case over Africa and view it all as history."

Looking across the compound, Fletch said, "Couldn't put Juma under a glass case. He'd break it."

"I believe he would," Carr said.

"By the way, Carr, I'm remembering that Barbara and I didn't take any medical shots before we left the States."

"You'll be all right," Carr said. "Be sure and take your whiskey." He glanced out to see where the sun was. "But, first, let's walk the riverbanks. I'll show you how far I haven't gotten with my crazy idea. Lost Roman city," Carr said. "Pah! I'm crazy!"

+++++++++++++++

"Last night I read the previous two days' newspaper reports on the murder you saw at the airport," Carr said as he and Fletch ambled along the riverbank. "I also talked with Dan Dawes."

"You talk to Dan Dawes?"

"Why not? He's a schoolteacher."

"He's also a paralegal executioner."

"That, too. Here we refer to him as being 'very close to the police.' "

"He's a hit man for the cops."

"There is great diversity in this world, Irwin. One must not expect the same standards everywhere."

"Sorry. Go on." As he walked, Fletch slapped at the flies on his arms, his legs.

"The murder victim's name was Louis Ramon. He was carrying a French passport. In a money belt he was also carrying an extraordinary amount of German marks—about one hundred thousand United States dollars' worth."

"He wasn't robbed?"

"No. They found the money on him."

Fletch marveled softly, "He wasn't even robbed by the police."

"Interpol's return cable said that Louis Ramon was some sort of a low-life currency trader, opportunist, possibly smuggler. He first came to their attention five years ago when he was suspected of moving a large amount of Italian lire into Switzerland, and again, three years ago, of moving a large amount of French francs into Albania. He has been fined and admonished, but has never served time in prison, as far as they know. Here, come this way. I'll show you what we're doing."

They turned right into the jungle and followed a track wide enough for a Jeep about twenty-five meters from the river. Foliage was beginning to overgrow the track.

At the end of the track they came to a circular clearing.

In the center of the clearing was a hole in the ground so small Fletch wouldn't have noticed it if it weren't for the settling mound of dirt surrounding it.

"We dig holes with a giant corkscrew," Carr said seriously, "see what comes up. What we use is actually a sort of primitive machine they use to look for water, before digging a well. We can only go down about fifteen meters. Do you think fifteen meters, forty-five feet, is enough to reach back two or three thousand years? I doubt it." He kicked the earth with his boot. "Soft earth. Jungle growth."

Carr led the way back toward the river. "Every hundred meters or so along the river, we go about twenty-five meters into the jungle and dig our little hole. Do you think that's far enough from the river? Too far? I think it's more likely a settlement would have been on the west side of the river, the inland side from the sea, don't you? We're apt to dig more holes anywhere there's an elevation in the land."

"How long have you been doing this?" Fletch asked.

"About eighteen months. Lots of holes, up and down both sides of the river."

They headed south along the river again.

"Anyway," Carr continued, "Louis Ramon was on your plane from London. The suspicion is that he came to Kenya to pull off some sort of a currency scheme, and his partner, or accomplice, or whoever he met at the airport in Nairobi, simply did him in."

"Not his partner," Fletch said. "Not his accomplice."

"Oh? Why not?"

"Because a partner or an accomplice would have known Ramon was carrying a hundred thousand dollars in German marks, and taken them. He had plenty of time. He wasn't that conscious that I was there. I mean, if you're going to stab someone in a men's room, you might as well rob him, right?"

"I forgot you're an investigative reporter," Carr said. "Old Josie Fletcher must be proud of you. You have her brain."

"I deal in reality, " Fletch muttered. They were passing another track into the jungle. "I think it was more of an accidental meeting. There was no prologue to the argument I heard. The voices were surprised. Immediately enraged. It was all very fast. It was as if two men met accidentally, two men who had known each other, hated each other before, had some ancient, powerful grudge between them, or maybe even saw each other as an immediate danger to each other, or one to the other. It was too fast," Fletch said. "I wish I understood Portuguese."

Carr was leading him up another jungle track.

In the clearing was what appeared certainly to be a giant corkscrew. An aluminum frame sat on the ground, four meters square at its base, one meter square at its top, about three meters tall. Sticking through it and twelve meters above it was a slim screw shaft. On each of the four sides of the frame was a wheel one meter in diameter with a perpendicular handle of the sort found on coffee grinders.

"I guess Sheila decided to backtrack," Carr said.

He stooped over the fresh mound of dirt and combed through it with his fingers. "Nothing. Do you think we're crazy?"

"What does it matter? Everyone's thought crazy until proven right."

Carr stood up and dusted off his hands. "Usually people are proven wrong, aren't they?"

"Yeah," Fletch said. "I guess most people are crazy."

"To choose your own way of being crazy," Carr said, stepping out again. "That's the thing."

When they were back walking the riverbank south, Fletch asked Carr, "How would such a currency scheme as Louis Ramon seemed to be attempting work?"

"I don't know," Carr said. "I'm not sure I want to know. But I do know that having that much foreign currency in Kenya is illegal."

"Why?"

"As far as its currency is concerned, Kenya's economy is closed. You may not take more than ten *shillingi* in Kenyan currency out of Kenya. The truth is, the Kenyan *shil-*

lingi doesn't exist outside Kenya. It's like casino money. It only has reality within its own closed environment. Kenyan money is pegged to the English pound, but there is no international trading or market in the currency itself."

"How do they manage that?"

"By strict enforcement of the law. A while ago, an Indian lawyer was discovered by the police to have thirteen United States dollars in his pocket. He was sentenced to seven years in prison for currency violations."

"I'd call that strict enforcement of the law."

"Let's cross the river here. Walk back on the other side."

They stripped. Carrying their clothes head high, they waded across the sluggish river. The water was armpit high on them both.

Carr said, "You can see all sorts of signs this river used to be deeper. Can't you?"

While they were waiting on the eastern riverbank to dry off, Carr glanced at the black and blue mark on Fletch's lower belly, but said nothing.

Carr pointed back across the river, further south. "See that baobab tree there? Tomorrow I think we'll make a trail into the jungle past that. But we mustn't disturb the tree. Baobab trees are sacred here. Rather than disturb them, people here build major highways around them."

After dressing, they walked faster northward along the riverbank. They ignored the many trails into the jungle.

"Kenyans take anything having to do with the government very seriously indeed," Carr said.

"Juma says his father is in prison for a year and a half for parking a government car outside a bar. He used to be a government driver."

"Not long ago," Carr said, "one of your fellow Americans had dinner in a Nairobi restaurant. Two men waited on him. At the end of dinner, the man wanted to tip them both, but he only had a one-hundred-*shillingi* note. I guess he thought he was making a joke. He tore the one-hundred-*shillingi* note in half and tried to give half to each waiter. The newspaper report I read said, 'Shocked and embarrassed at this desecration of Kenyan money, the waiters called the police.' The man was arrested. He spent the night in jail. He was tried the next morning, fined one thousand dollars, and escorted by the police to the airport and put aboard the next airplane leaving Kenya."

"Some joke."

"It's illegal, of course," Carr said, "but here, in the bush, girls are still circumcised. But you tear a piece of paper money in half and you get yourself written up in *The Standard.*"

Fletch asked, "So how would you work a currency scheme?"

Carr walked a long way before answering. "Generally it's true," he said slowly, "that the stricter such currency laws are, the greater are the rewards for violating them successfully."

The camp came into sight just at full dark. The live fire at the back of the cook tent was bright.

As they were wading back across the river, Carr said, "I guess we're crazy. Looking for a lost Roman city. But the past fascinates. Doesn't the past fascinate you? The past, where we came from, who we were, tells us so much about who we are. Don't you think so?"

Fletch ducked below the surface of the water to get some of the sweat out of his hair.

While they were drying on the western riverbank, Carr said, "I guess I'm just messing up the jungle."

"Not much."

"I've promised myself one thing, though." He was looking downriver. "The instant I find anything, the slightest evidence I'm right, if I ever do, I'll turn the whole thing over to proper scientists. If I'm right, I swear I won't muck the site up."

"Right," Fletch said. "What this place needs is Dr. McCoy. You won't catch him clipping off anybody's toes."

"As soon as you and Barbara are ready," Carr said, "join us for a whiskey. Bring your own ice."

Conversationally, Sheila said to Barbara, "You're enjoying your honeymoon?"

"He drives me nuts."

"Yes. There's always that."

They were sitting in a semicircle in camp chairs just outside the long stretch of canvas on four poles. Carr had provided each with a Scotch and soda. Bug-repellent candles were here and there around them. Over them hung a moon such as Fletch had never seen before. It was a black orb within a perfect silver circumference. The noises from the jungle were absolutely raucous. As he listened to the conversation, Fletch watched the monkeys playing about here and there in the candlelight. Under the canvas behind them, a man named Winston had set the dining table for four.

"He complains I speak nicely to him in public and nastily to him in private," Barbara said.

"There's a lot of that goes on in marriage," Sheila said.

Carr said, "We're not exactly married."

"So I've decided to speak nastily to him in public, too." Barbara giggled.

"Will you speak nicely to me in private?" Fletch asked.

"If there is ever anything to speak nicely to you about, I will say it both in public and in private."

Juma came out of the dark carrying a camp chair. He sat down with them.

Carr asked, "Would you like a whiskey, Juma?"

"No. Thank you. I don't like whiskey. It makes me drunk."

"Oh. I see."

Fletch said to Sheila, "Our honeymoon has not worked out as planned."

"Barbara mentioned something about your planning a skiing honeymoon. In Colorado."

"She did?" Fletch mocked surprise.

"Yes. She did mention it."

"Our wedding was not as planned, either," Barbara said. "It was on a bluff overlooking the Pacific Ocean. Fletch was late. The wedding got rained out. He spent the day with his mother."

Carr shot Fletch a quick glance.

"Weddings aren't all they're cracked up to be," Fletch advised Carr. "You haven't missed much."

"He showed up at his wedding in blue jeans, a well-used T-shirt, and torn sneakers."

"I'd shaved. You must understand, I'd been working day and night. I have a job."

Juma leaned close to Fletch and asked quietly, "Is Barbara your first wife?"

Fletch blinked. "Yes."

"Oh, I see."

"Clothes don't make the couple," Sheila said. "At least, not until later in life."

Carr said, "You both look hot."

Because of the flies, Barbara and Fletch had decided to wear long ski pants, sweaters with sleeves, and ski boots to dinner.

"I'm boiling," Barbara said. "Are you sure you're not having me for dinner?"

They had been surprised to find Sheila and Carr dressed only in pajamas and mosquito boots.

"Dining in pajamas is an old Kenyan custom," Carr said. "A natural result of *safarini*. After spending a day in the bush, the thing you most want, after a drink, is a bath. After a bath, what's more natural than slipping into cool, cotton pajamas? They even look more formal than our usual short-pants rig. In the bad old days, people used to go dine at each other's houses in pajamas. They'd even go out to dine at a hotel or restaurant in pajamas."

Close by, a lion roared.

"Good God!" Barbara said. "I'm being boiled for a lion!"

"Think of it as a tape recording, if you wish," Carr said.

"I shall be eaten alive."

"Whatever shall I tell your mother?" Fletch asked.

"No, no," Carr said. "Hungry lions are quiet lions. That roar sounds like he's had his kill, his fill, his sleep, and now he's calling around to see where his pride is, where his friends are." Either the lion roared more loudly, or the lion was closer. "Your average wild beast has seen man and doesn't think much of us."

"Even as dessert?" Barbara asked.

"Even as a snack."

A man named Raffles came by to freshen their drinks.

"We came out to Africa to meet my father," Fletch said to Sheila. "At our wedding a man showed up with a letter from him."

"A letter written in disappearing ink," Barbara added.

"Yes," Sheila said. "Peter told me there'd been some trouble at the Thorn Tree Café. It doesn't sound too serious."

Fletch looked at Juma. "It sounds to me that any trouble with the law in Kenya is very serious."

"A wonderfully attractive man, your father," Sheila said.

"He is?" Carr asked.

"Don't you think so?"

"No."

"A little immature, perhaps. But some societies prize immaturity in a man."

"Irresponsible," said Carr. "When he was flying for me, I never knew where the hell he was."

"Well," Sheila admitted, "he is a bit of a will-o'-the-wisp."

Barbara said, "I'll say."

"Enormously popular," Sheila said.

"Maybe with the ladies," Carr said.

"Oh, come on, Peter. You men like him, too."

Carr shook his head. "Too much the iconoclast."

Sheila said, "He does have his own way of doing things. But, after all, most of the people who have settled in Africa have done so because they're a bit too individualistic for other places. Take you, for example, Peter."

"Right," said Carr. "I have my own way of doing things. But usually I stay out of the beds of other chaps' wives, and keep my fists out of other chaps' faces."

Fletch winced. "How come you're friends?"

There was a moment before Carr answered. "What are friends? The international fraternity of fliers. Roughly the same age. We find ourselves in the same place at the same time."

Sheila said, "Walter Fletcher is a man of great personal energy."

"Mostly misspent," Carr muttered.

"Why do you say that?" Sheila asked. "He has his own plane, plenty of work—"

"There's a reverse spin to everything he does," Carr said. "He flies in our faces, is what he does. Last year, as a group, we decided to stop flying in and out of Uganda. Too much paperwork. Too dangerous for our equipment and passengers. Your Walter Fletcher takes to flying in and out of Uganda like a hawk. Makes three years' pay in one year, at least." Looking at the moon, Carr asked, "And where is he now?"

"But you came with him to the hotel," Fletch said, "to meet us."

"Exactly," Carr said. "I was there, and he wasn't."

"You said you were there to be his moral support."

"Right." Carr put down his glass. "Walter's morals need propping up. Care to eat with us, Juma?"

Juma glanced at Sheila. "No, thank you. I've eaten."

In the candlelight, Carr was looking into Fletch's eyes. "All this has nothing to do with you, you know."

Fletch said, "Oh. I see."

+++++++++++++++

"Will you be able to spend a few days with us, Peter?" Sheila asked.

"A few days. Then I have to fly some French *hôteliers* up to the Masai Mara. Pick them up in Nairobi. They're traveling around, studying the Block Hotels. I'll be gone two nights."

"The Masai Mara," Fletch said. "I hear it's nice there."

"Welcome to join me," Carr said. "There'll be room in the plane."

"If we don't hear from Walter first," Sheila said.

"Yeah. I told his lawyer where we'd all be."

"Who flies your other plane?" Fletch asked.

"A young Kenyan. He's flying hard for us these days, while I'm down here wasting time and money. The perks of age and ownership. He can't make the Masai Mara trip, though. He's chartered to fly to Madagascar."

"I'm afraid we're imposing," said Fletch.

"Why? Good company is worth anything in the bush. Tomorrow we'll all get some hard work in."

"Would you rather be sitting in a hotel room in Nairobi?" Sheila asked.

For the fifth time, Barbara waved flies away from her rice.

"Went to see the witch doctor of Thika, old dear," Carr said to Sheila. "Barbara and young Irwin here came with me. Actually, that's where Juma attached himself to us, too."

"Was she encouraging?" Sheila's gold bracelets jangled as she ate.

"Right on. Straightaway, she said I was looking for something I hadn't lost. When I said it was a place, she said I must go south where there are hills and a river."

"That's where we are," Sheila said.

"She said the people who used to live here want us to find their place, so they'll be remembered."

"Did she say we will find it?"

"Definitely yes."

Sheila said, "At this point, encouragement from any source is welcome."

In the cook tent, a tape of a contemporary Italian love song was playing. Juma and Winston and Raffles and the five or six other young men behind the tent were lustily and perfectly singing the lyrics, in Italian.

Fletch couldn't be sure if some of the bird noises he was hearing were from the tape or from the jungle around them. They, too, matched or followed the music perfectly.

++++++++++++++

"Barbara? Stand up, please?"

After dinner they had returned to their camp chairs in front of the dining awning. Carr had poured them each a Three Barrels brandy.

Juma appeared dressed now with just a cloth wrapped high around his waist. He was carrying an unfolded cotton cloth about four feet by five and a half feet.

Even in the candlelight, the reds, greens, yellows of both cloths were bright.

"Ah, Juma, the perfect solution!" Sheila said. "A *kanga!*"

Juma ignored her.

Whcn Barbara stood up, Juma wrapped the cloth around her, under her armpits, over her breasts, and tied it to itself, simply.

It was a full, free-hanging dress.

Barbara looked down at herself. "Far out!"

"Beats jodhpurs," Fletch said.

Juma slipped it off her and folded it lengthwise. He put it around her hips like a sling. Holding the two ends together with one hand, he ran his finger against both sides of the cloth up against her waist. He used that point as the fold. He tucked the top end of the cloth into the cloth itself against her other hip.

It was a skirt.

"That's all you need wear around here."

"Nothing on top?" Barbara asked.

"I can get you some necklaces, too, if you like."

Again he slipped the cloth off her. This time he folded it lengthwise in quarters and tucked it around her waist again, finding the fold with his fingers.

It was a short skirt.

"Very cool," Juma said.

Looking below the skirt to her thighs, knees in ski pants, Barbara said, "I'll say."

"It goes well with your ski boots," Fletch said.

"Also," Juma said, "as you see, a man can wear a *kanga.* Stand up, please, Fletch."

Fletch put his glasss of brandy on the ground beside his chair and stood up.

Juma draped the *kanga* over Fletch's shoulders. "Keeps off the sunbite," Juma said.

Then he folded the *kanga* in quarters again and using the same method tucked it around Fletch's waist.

There was the sound of a burp.

Holding the glass to his face with both hands, a monkey was finishing Fletch's brandy.

"Hold on." Carr got up abruptly. "Better restrain that fellow until the brandy wears off." He began to approach the monkey slowly. "No telling what he might do."

Barbara said, "Just like your father, Fletch."

Juma tugged the *kanga* off Fletch's waist and handed it to Barbara.

"For me? A present?"

"Yes," Juma said. "I got it for you. So you will be dressed right, and be cool."

"How nice," Sheila said.

The monkey had put down the glass. He scratched the top of his head.

"Thank you, Juma."

When Carr was almost ready to pounce on the monkey, the monkey suddenly laughed and darted away. He scrambled up the banyan tree.

Hands on hips, Carr watched the monkey climb high into the tree. "Now what do we do?"

"Can you see him?" Barbara asked.

Using only one hand, chattering wildly, the monkey was swinging from a branch ten meters above the ground.

"Come down here, you silly bastard," Carr said. "Do you suppose we can coax him down with a little more brandy?"

The monkey scrambled even higher. He was now fifteen meters off the ground. Putting one foot in front of the other, holding his arms out for balance, he teetered out a long branch like a tightrope walker. Looking down at them, he chattered a fairly long speech.

"He'll hurt himself," Sheila said.

"More than likely," Carr agreed.

"The whiskey made the monkey drunk, you see," Juma said.

The monkey stepped off the tree branch backward. He caught himself with both hands.

Using both arms, the monkey began swinging from the tree branch, swinging higher and higher.

"Oh, dear," Carr said. "I'm afraid he means to give us a flying lesson."

At the highest point of his swing, with no destination discernable, the monkey let go of the branch. He went up into the air feet first in a perfect arc.

Carr sprinted forward. "Can we catch him?"

In a great puff of dust, the monkey landed on his back a meter in front of Carr.

In the inflection of the disappointed, the monkey said, "Ohhhhh."

"Bastard knocked himself out," Carr said. "That'll teach him to fly too far too high too fast."

They were all looking down at the monkey unconscious on the ground.

"He will have a headache," Juma prophesied.

Fletch said to Barbara, *"Just like my father!!?"*

29

After gazing, not really looking, into the jungle for several minutes while taking a water/rest break from his work, Fletch jumped.

A young man was looking back at him.

The young man stood perfectly still on one leg. His other foot was off the ground. His body was in profile but his head was turned to look full-faced at Fletch. Extremely tall, extremely thin, the young man's body was an upright black stick among the foliage. He wore a feathered head-dress. His earlobes had been opened and extended. They hung nearly to his shoulders. Over one shoulder he wore a strip of cloth which joined the narrow strip somehow around his waist. Bracelets were around the muscles of his arms. His anklets were red. His fingers loosely held a spear upright against his body.

"Hey!" Fletch said in suprise. "Hello!"

The young man did not speak or move.

"Jambo!" Fletch said. *"Habari?"*

Nothing.

Fletch held up his gallon jug of water. *"Magi baridi?"*

No response.

The young man stared at him silently, unmoving.

Fletch waved at him and went back to work.

With a *panga* he was cutting a trail wide enough through the light brush for the Jeep, from the riverbank into the jungle. He had not disturbed the baobab tree. Barefooted, in his swimming trunks, he worked alone.

Carr had told him never to take a step without looking carefully for snakes. During the morning, Fletch avoided a half dozen.

That morning Carr and the others were extending the path along the riverbank. The trees along the river were bigger, older, heavier. The ground needed filling in. That job required more of a team effort.

Doing this mindless work alone in the jungle, sweating profusely, felt good to Fletch. Besides lovemaking, his body had been confined too long to chairs and airplane seats, strange beds, the newspaper office. Since receiving the letter from his father the day of his wedding Fletch's mind had been belted with the unexpected too regularly: the conversation with his mother; flying out to Kenya; seeing the bloody, murdered man at the airport; his father not showing up; some of the things Barbara had taken to saying and doing. He did not understand the jungle noises, but he found them soothing. He admired the birds, as they came and went. He watched for snakes and cleared a path through the brush.

During the morning, whenever Fletch would stop to straighten his back, drink some water, which was frequently, he would look at the young man standing silently, watching. The young man was more still, more unmoving, than any animate object Fletch had ever seen. Standing still for a long period is the hardest exercise. Being so still, first on one leg, then on the other, took great discipline. Fletch never saw him change his weight from one leg to the other. Why was the young man posing this way?

During his first few breaks, Fletch would hold up his water bottle in offering to the young man, then wave at him before going back to work.

But as the morning wore on and Fletch found himself thinking about this and that, *"Running for Love"* humming in his mind, he forgot the young man was there. Gazing around, Fletch's eyes would not pick out the still figure unless he remembered him and focused on him. The young man's silence, stillness, made him drop from consciousness, almost disappear from view.

Juma spotted him immediately.

Late morning, Fletch heard Juma coming down the trail Fletch had cut. He was whistling that Italian love song. From one hand dangled a full gallon of water.

"Fletch must drink plenty of water," Juma said. "Fletch is not used to this heat. Fletch is not used to this work. Fletch comes from America, where the hardest work is pushing buttons."

Juma's body was as soaked with sweat as Fletch's.

Juma put the fresh jug of water on the ground. Looking up, he saw the young man standing on the knoll.

"Ug!" Immediately, Juma grabbed up two handfuls of dirt. He flung one handful in the direction of the young man. "Idiot!" He started toward the young man. Closer, he threw the other handful of dirt. "Go away! What do you think you're doing? Stupid!"

Juma stooped to pick up a stick.

His eyes now on Juma, the young man stepped sideways into the jungle. Immediately the foliage covered him.

"Son of a bitch!" Juma yelled after him. "Why don't you come into this century!" Turning back to Fletch, Juma said, "At least this half of the century." He dropped the stick.

"I wanted to see how long he'd stay that way."

Juma waved his hand. "For the rest of his life. He'd die that way."

"Why was he doing it?"

"Who knows? Who cares? Some of these people live in another world. They know about radios, telephones. Tiresome. Someone that age . . ."

"Thanks for bringing me the water."

Juma picked up the empty jug. "Carr said he'll be along later, with your lunch." Juma began to walk down the trail. "Go ahead. Eat in the midday. It will make you more hot, more tired, sweat more. You Europeans insist on consuming and wasting, consuming and wasting, just to keep yourselves sick."

The young man with the spear did not return, that Fletch could see, or feel.

✦✦✦✦✦✦✦✦✦✦✦✦✦✦✦

Fletch was hungry for lunch well before Carr arrived.

They sat cross-legged on the ground in the center of a wide bare spot. They ate fish sandwiches with a third jug of water.

For all the water Fletch was drinking, he was urinating little.

Carr said, "I thought you'd appreciate a morning working alone."

"I enjoyed it."

Fletch told Carr about the young man who had spent much of the morning at silent attention watching him. And that Juma had come along and chased him away.

"Sounds like a Masai *moran*. A warrior. A *mti*. An *mtii*. They're not allowed to carry shields anymore."

"Why did he carry a spear?"

"Because of the snakes."

"Sounds sensible. Maybe I should carry a spear."

"Pretty far south for a Masai these days. But you never can tell. They're nomads. Follow the grazing."

"What tribe is Juma's?"

"I'm pretty sure he's Kikuyu. There are over forty tribes in East Africa."

"And over all these centuries the tribes have remained segregated enough, distinct enough, so that you can tell one from the other?"

"Pretty much so. To this point in history, the political struggles in Africa have almost nothing to do with ideologies, East versus West, socialism versus free enterprise, communism versus capitalism. The struggles for power are among the tribes. Wish you'd tell your chaps in Washington that."

"I'll write them a letter."

"There's even a tribe near here which denies it exists. No one but its own members knows its true name. You meet a member of that tribe and he will always tell you he's a member of some other tribe. Prove to him he's not, and he'll say, 'Well . . .' and insist he is a member of even another tribe. They're a secret tribe. They camouflage themselves among all the other tribes. The true name of the tribe may be the Wata."

"Sure." Fletch grinned. "Wata tribe. I got it."

"You don't believe me?"

"Was Juma working with you this morning?"

"Yes."

"Are you paying him?"

"Am I paying you?"

"No."

Carr smiled. "You're working off that mosquito net you and Barbara wrecked last night."

"Oh." Fletch scratched his elbow. "You know about that."

"Raffles mentioned to Sheila this morning that someone will have to spend a day sewing."

"Sorry about that."

"There is a technique to doing what you want to do under mosquito netting. You'll learn."

"So why is Juma working for you if he's not being paid?"

"I don't know. I didn't ask him to come with us. I didn't ask him to work. I guess he just wants to be with us."

"Are you paying the other men?"

"Of course."

"Why does Juma want to be with us?"

"Perhaps because he loves you?"

"Loves who?"

"Loves you. Loves Barbara. Do I mean love? He's very curious about you both. He watches you very closely, how you walk, how you talk, relate to each other, and others, what and when you eat, drink, how you dress, what your bodies are like and how you use them, your minds."

"I'm curious about Juma, too."

"It's a very dear relationship, if you find you can relate to it at all decently. He's interested, but uncritical. Can you understand that?"

"The other night, standing on the sidewalk outside the Norfolk, he said something which totally baffled Barbara and me. He said he doesn't decide who are his friends and who are not his friends. He said something like making such decisions is very *hard*, but he may have meant very *harsh*."

"Generally very uncritical," Carr repeated.

"He certainly made a fast decision about the young man with the spear standing in the bush over there. Instantly, he picked up things and started throwing them at him. He swore at him."

"Yeah. Well. A modern young man like Juma is apt to have great impatience with other people, especially people his own age, who cling to tribal ways. They don't like that spear-shaking image of Africa."

More quietly, Fletch said, "He certainly seems to have made a rather harsh decision about Sheila."

"Yes," Carr said. "He inherited that. There is a distinct prejudice here against people of East Indian extraction."

"Why?"

"Throughout Africa, throughout much of the third world in fact, Indians own most of the *duccas*, the stores. They do most of the trading, the buying and selling. Therefore, the native populations think the Indians have an disproportionate share of the goods and the money."

"Do they feel the Indians exploit them?"

"Don't we all feel a little exploited by the shopkeeper? We give him more money for something than he paid for it, and we know it. Then, with his profits, the shopkeeper goes off and builds a house better than any we could afford. Trouble is, some of the poorest Africans I know are of East Indian extraction. Some of the richest, too. Sheila was born in Kenya. She was a workingwoman when I met her. She worked for a car rental agency."

"So Juma crosses her off completely, as a Kenyan, as a woman, as a person."

Carr shrugged. "Prejudice is like that. Are you surprised to find prejudice in Africa?"

Fletch had finished his lunch. "Carr, I went to the jail yesterday."

Carr's eyebrows shot up. "Oh?"

"To see my father."

"They let you in?"

"They would have. My father sent out the message that he wasn't in."

"Cute."

"I thought so."

"Can't fault old Fletcher for his humor."

"At least I proved one thing to myself."

"What's that?"

"There is a Walter Fletcher."

"Did you doubt that?"

Fletch removed a speck from his eye. "I think Barbara was beginning to hope you are my father."

Carr laughed. "I'm flattered."

"We came to meet my father, you see, and we met you instead."

Carr refolded the brown paper in which he had brought lunch. "If you keep cuttin' trail, I'll go get the corkscrew."

"So I know Walter Fletcher exists," Fletch said, "which I really didn't know before." He sighed. "And for once in my life, I know exactly where he is."

"Hapana kitu."

Barbara and Carr knelt on the ground watching the soil as it came up the screw to the surface. Sheila stood over them, arms akimbo, watching, saying nothing.

On the four sides of the earth screw's frame, Juma, Fletch, Winston, and Raffles turned the wheels sending the screw into the ground. For the most part, the earth was soft. Forcing the screw slowly into the ground wasn't very hard work.

Carr's fingers crumbled a piece of rotten wood that surfaced. "Nothing," he repeated.

An hour or so after Carr had left Fletch, the derelict-looking Jeep snorted up the trail Fletch had cleared. Looking huge and ridiculous, the aluminum corkscrew stuck far out of the back of the Jeep. Twelve meters behind the Jeep men carried the top of the shaft. Barbara, wearing her *kanga*, rode in the Jeep with Carr.

The rest, including Sheila, walked beside the Jeep.

It seemed an invasion of the solitude Fletch had enjoyed in the jungle.

It was fairly easy, tipping the corkscrew up and making it even on the ground.

The top of the screw shaft reached its lowest point. The wheels could turn no further.

"Right," Carr said. "Bring it up."

It was easier, unscrewing the earth.

They continued to watch what earth came up with the screw.

"Pity we're not in the well-drilling business," Carr said. "At least sometimes we find water."

"Ever find oil?" Fletch asked.

"Not even hair grease."

Wrestling the corkscrew around, they tried three other places in that clearing that afternoon. Fletch tried a few pleasantries until he realized they weren't appreciated. They didn't find a lost Roman city, but he had enjoyed the day.

"*Hapana kitu*," Carr said. "Nothing. Let's go back to camp. There's always tomorrow."

"Hello," Juma said. "Stay where the crocodiles are used to us. They are very territorial, you see."

Naked, Barbara and Fletch were swimming in the river.

Naked, Juma sat on a rock in the river watching them.

"Crocodiles?" Barbara stood up in the river.

"Haven't you seen them?" Fletch asked.

"Crocodiles that eat people?"

"I don't think they're particular."

"Fletch," Barbara whispered. "Juma's naked."

"So are we."

"What does he mean? That there's nothing *sexual* between us? Among us?"

"I'll ask him."

"Screw crocodiles." Barbara started for the riverbank in haste. "Never even got to wash my hair."

Fletch climbed up onto the rock and sat beside Juma.

"Barbara wants to know if there's nothing *sexual* among us."

"What does she mean?"

"Among us three, I guess she means. You and her."

"Barbara wants a baby by me? That would be odd."

"No. She doesn't. We three were just naked together."

"People put on clothes to be sexual, don't they?"

"People do many things to be sexual."

"What else are clothes for?"

"Pockets."

Juma was rubbing the fingers of his right hand against his leg. "Africans don't have pockets. We have nothing to put in them." The red stain on his fingers was not coming off. "People can be sexual with each other whether they wear clothes or not."

"True."

Juma was looking at the mark on the lower right side of Fletch's stomach. Juma said, "So you are partly black."

"And blue."

"I have never seen such a thing before. Is that the way a baby would look, if Barbara and I had a baby? I don't think so."

"No."

"It looks odd."

"Black people do not turn white where they are hit."

"Who hit you? Did someone in Kenya hit you?"

"Why are your fingers red?"

"*Miraa.*"

"What's *miraa?*"

"You don't know *miraa?* It's a drug we chew. A pleasure drug."

"Like marijuana?"

"What's marijuana?"

"A pleasure drug."

"It leaves the fingers red, and the gums and tongue." Juma showed Fletch how red his gums and tongue were. "Also, I suppose, our insides. It's not very good. One of the men gave me some." Juma nodded up the riverbank toward the cook tent. "You can buy some in any store which has banana leaves over the door."

"I read some of that book you lent me, *Weep Not Child*."

Juma snorted. "Ngugi blames white people for almost everything."

"Including inventing war."

"As if they were gods." Juma put his hand on the back of Fletch's neck and squeezed. "Are you a god, Fletch?"

"Tell me about my father."

"He's all right." Juma returned to trying to rub the red stain off his fingers. "A bit of a *mutata*."

"What's *mutata*?"

"Troublesome."

"He's a nuisance?"

Juma laughed. "Once he rode into Narok on his motorcycle, slowly, slowly, dragging behind him with a rope around its neck a hyena."

"He still rides a motorcycle."

"He insisted some people bet him the night before he could not lasso a hyena and bring it into Narok by the second hour of daylight the next day." Juma laughed again. "Trouble was, no one remembered having made such a bet with him. No one would admit to such a bet."

"He sounds crazy."

"It's all right. No one likes hyenas much."

There was a particularly loud chattering from the jungle across the river.

"Juma, when Carr took me to Lake Turkana he told me there's an elephant skeleton, very, very old, buried near there, at Koobi Fora."

"Of course it's very old, if it's a skeleton."

"The skeleton of an East Indian elephant."

"Buried in East Africa?"

"It didn't swim across the Indian Ocean."

Juma thought a moment. "You're talking about Carr's woman."

"Her name is Sheila."

"Well, her skeleton will belong in India."

"She was born in Kenya. In Lamû."

"All the borders are colonial. Have you thought that? The borders of all these nations were set by the English and the Germans and the French, not by the tribes."

"I like Sheila. I like Carr."

"Perhaps while you are here, I will take you to Shimoni."

"What's Shimoni?"

"It means hole-in-the-ground. It's a place on the coast. I have been there."

"Sheila worked for a car rental agency when Carr first met her."

"Perhaps you and I will go to a three-in-one hotel."

"What's a three-in-one hotel?"

"You have never been to one?"

"I don't think so."

"Three in one bed. They are very popular here. I think they are very good especially for a man who must treat one wife at a time."

"I see. Are you married, Juma?"

"No. I want to go to school. I want to work in television. Don't you think it would be very good to work in television?"

"Yes. I do."

"What is your work?" Juma asked.

"I work for a newspaper."

"Oh, I see. That would be interesting work. Somewhat the same work as television, I think, except no one can see your face. If you are going to tell people something, don't you think you should say it so people can see your face?"

"I believe it is easier to find out what to tell people if they do not see your face."

"Oh, I see. Yes, perhaps that is true." Juma stood up on the rock. "Well, it is time for you to go have your Scotch whiskey."

"Why?"

Juma shrugged. "You had a Scotch whiskey last night at this time."

"They adore him."

"Who?"

"Carr. The women just eat him up."

Carr was having an after-dinner beer at the lodge's bar with the two women *hôtelières* they had flown up from Nairobi. Carr was sitting sideways to the bar on a stool. The two French women stood with their drinks, facing him. They laughed at everything he said.

Barbara and Fletch were drinking beer at a small table at the side of the veranda.

At the entrance to the veranda, a guard with a flashlight and rifle waited to escort the tourists to their cabins.

"Don't you find Carr attractive?" Fletch asked.

Barbara looked around at the few remaining tourists who had not yet gone to bed.

"Every woman in the place," Barbara said, "is just eating him up."

After clearing trails and digging holes and finding nothing significant one more day, Barbara, Fletch, and Carr had flown to Nairobi, refueled, picked the two women up, and then flown west to the Masai Mara.

Sheila said she preferred to stay in camp and dig holes along the freshly cut trails. She promised she would find a Roman city before they returned.

There was no discussion about whether Juma would accompany them. While they were getting ready to go, he simply did not appear.

The two women hotel executives from France were *très chic, très jolie*. They were on a business trip, but they were also having a good time. They handed around a bottle of champagne on the airplane. Carr did not drink any.

They marveled happily flying over the Rift Valley, the Loita Hills and Plains, ecologically the Serengeti Plains. Carr flew as low as he decently, legally could, so they could all see the herds of zebras, elands, giraffes grazing. The older woman, who sat in the copilot seat, snapped photographs from the air with a little camera genuinely useless at the distance of more than three meters. She thought she was getting wonderful pictures. Their first sight of elephants from the air sent them into raptures. In fast, stuttering English they were full of questions for Carr.

The women were warmly greeted by management and immediately taken on a tour of Keekorok Lodge. Even Fletch wondered how a lodge so far in the bush could provide such impeccable food and drink, accommodations and service.

Carr organized a *safari guari* and driver. That night and the next day, sunrise and sunset, while the hotel executives studied the operation of the lodge, Carr, Barbara, and Fletch toured the reserve.

They were to be at the lodge only two nights, before returning to Nairobi, and then Carr's camp.

The *safari guari* was a well-spirited, well-sprung, fairly quiet Nissan van, roofless so they could stand in it, the clean, bush-scented African-air wind in their faces, so they could see all sides at once from an elevation of three meters as they rode along. Carr provided binoculars for them. They learned to brace themselves against the van's frame so they could use the binoculars reasonably well as they joggled along. They also learned from the driver, Omoke, a Kisi, a new way of looking at landscape, of surveying vast areas quickly, mathematically, with just their eyes, going over it in sideways Z's, spotting anything moving, anything even slightly outstanding in color. Anything remarkable spotted Omoke would drive to, through the bush, quietly, drawing up and stopping at a decent, noninterfering, nonmeddling distance.

Almost immediately Omoke found for them a lion and two lionesses sprawled in the fading sunlight. The tail and the hind legs of the lion were embraced by the forelegs of one lioness; his head and one shoulder were on the shoulder of the other lioness. Their heads were up. They were looking around lazily, the light from the low sun in their eyes. The bellies of all three were so stuffed they lay on the ground almost separately, like suitcases.

Before sunrise the next morning, Omoke, who saw a landscape differently from any painter, any engineer, found a small grassy depression in the ground in the shade of a bush. Lying in the hollow, clearly exhausted, was a cheetah who, just hours before, had given birth to four.

Later that afternoon they watched this same cheetah on uncertain legs hunt, bring down and kill an eland, to feed on and to feed her young. Immediately, hyenas came and took her kill from her. They dragged it a few meters away and devoured it.

The cheetah sat, blinking in the sunlight, watching them, clearly too tired to protest, to go on, just yet, or to go back, foodless, to her young.

From the ground, even more than the beasts, the dik-diks, the zebras, Thompson's and Grant's gazelles, topis, tree and rock hyraxes, impalas, leopards, lions, waterbucks, elephants, giraffes, or, down by the Mara River, the vervet monkeys, patas monkeys, olive baboons, were the birds, big and small, fascinating, the marabou storks and sacred ibises, secretary birds, Egyptian vultures, black kites, peregrines, francolins, spur fowl, bustards, plovers, turacos, the white-bellied go-away birds. Omoke had a bird book which he passed around. He knew his birds, but it was fun for Barbara and Fletch to look from this amazing bird in the bush to the book to confirm that such a creature existed and had a name and that one could believe one's eyes.

Besides these specific observations, the general observation of African arithmetic is impressive. The social unit of many, if not most, species of birds and beasts is dominated by a single male. He has two wives, five wives, ten wives, fifty wives, seventy wives. Besides bearing the children, the wives do the work of hunting and feeding. All these wives and children belong to the single male, at least as long as he can fight off whatever young male would like to take his place. The only way this stupefying arithmetic can work out is if a shocking number of young males die trying. Or so Barbara and Fletch worked out in the back of the *guari*.

Giraffes stretch their long necks to graze off the top of trees, their four slim legs, bodies, long, graceful necks making something architectural out of whatever tree they graze/grace.

On the way back to the lodge that second night, they stopped to watch elephants graze through a stand of long, coarse grass. An elephant uses its tusk like a spoon, its trunk like a fork. With its tusk, an elephant digs down into the earth, loosens and lifts whatever it is eating. His trunk grabs it and swings it into his mouth, grass, root, soil, all together, all the while making this wonderful, rhythmical swaying movement, as if inviting someone to dance, or to box.

"The women are giving up," Barbara said. At the bar, the two French hotel executives had put down their empty glasses. "They are going to bed. Seeing we need an *askari* to escort us, I might as well leave with them."

"Okay. I'll have a nightcap with Carr."

After she stood up, Barbara said, "You might not find your father on this trip. But it looks to me as if you may have found your father figure."

"Barbara says every woman around is eating you up with her eyes," Fletch said.

Carr had brought two fresh beers to the table. "Occupational hazard. Women can think bush pilots attractive, but, for the most part, they'd never think of marrying one." He touched his glass to Fletch's. "Home tomorrow to the camp, and Sheila."

They drank.

Fletch said, "Barbara and I are very grateful to you, Mr. Peter Carr. Seeing the Masai Mara has been a most memorable treat."

"Then perhaps you'll permit me a personal question?"

"Of course."

Carr took another swallow of his beer before speaking. "You've got me a bit confused, young Fletcher. I'm speaking of the murder you saw, or half saw, at the airport."

"Yes."

"I understand your not running out of the men's room yelling bloody murder, or I guess I do. Jet-lagged, deeply shocked, sick, newly arrived in a country foreign to you, knowing no one here, unsure of your father, his invitation, all that."

"Did he ever indicate to you he might meet us at the airport?"

"But in the days since then, why haven't you come forward? Granted, the authorities here would want you to testify, might hold you over, and, sooner rather than later you want to get back to your own lives in the States . . . but something could be worked out, don't you think?"

Fletch cleared his throat. "My ace in the hole."

"You're playing poker?"

"There are those who say life is poker."

"What's in the pot?"

"My father."

"Oh, I see. I think I see."

"I'm talking about a trade-off, Carr."

Carr's eyes narrowed. "The senior Fletcher for a murderer."

"Carr, I've been listening to you all. That's what a reporter does: he listens. I'm in a country, however you love it, where a tourist is jailed, fined, and expelled for tearing a hundred-*shillingi* note in half; where a government driver is jailed for eighteen months for parking a government car outside a bar; where an Indian lawyer is sentenced to seven years in prison for having thirteen U.S. dollars in his pocket. My father got into a drunken bar brawl and may or may not have slugged a cop. What's that worth in Kenyan prison time?"

"I see. You're looking forward to doing a deal."

"If it comes to it, I know a deal is possible. No police in the world would fail to forgive what is essentially a misdemeanor for an eyewitness account of a murder."

"You're not just playing Hamlet."

"I see my father's ghost, and that's about all."

Quietly, Carr said, "You don't even know the chap."

"He's my father."

"And that means something to you?"

"I don't know what it means to me."

"He ran off on you and your mother. He seems to have ignored you all your life. A few days ago, in prison, he refused to see you."

"Am I crazy?"

"I don't know."

"He also arranged for Barbara and me to come out here to meet him, spend some time with him, get to know him. There must be some feeling there. At least 'mild curiosity.' "

"There's a moral question here somewhere."

"Is there? How do I know what morals there are within a family, between a father and a son? No one ever taught me."

"I see."

"I know I don't want to see anyone who is my father spend months, years in an African prison for getting pissed and blindly swinging out at someone."

"Not quite what I mean. You can identify a murderer, someone who has murdered and is still at large."

"You mean you think he may murder again?"

"Exactly. Don't you have the responsibility to get the chap off the streets?"

Fletch shook his head. "No. That was a murder of impulse, of rage. I was there."

"The police aren't so sure," Carr said. "I made a phone call while we were in Nairobi."

"Dan Dawes?"

"The same."

Fletch chuckled. "The police informant."

"Right. The police inform him of everything. Bringing hard currency into Kenya isn't illegal; in fact, it's rather appreciated. Failing to declare the money upon arrival is illegal. In getting as far as the men's room without declaring this extraordinary number of *deutsche marks*, Louis Ramon, who, by the way, was on your airplane, had committed a crime."

"So?"

"So the Kenyan police are looking for a Kenyan financial acrobat who had desperate need for that much hard currency."

"Wrong. The man who killed, what's-his-name, Louis Ramon?"

"Right."

"Was not the man Louis Ramon came to meet. Whoever killed Louis Ramon did not know he was carrying one hundred thousand dollars in hard currency on him. You can't tell me someone's willing to do murder and not willing to stoop over and pick up one hundred thousand dollars if he knows it's there."

"Dan thought that point interesting."

"Was Dan interested in why you called?"

"Beg pardon?"

"Carr, in calling Dan Dawes, you're showing a lot of interest in a case which has nothing to do with you. Aren't you afraid of making him, and the police, suspicious of you?"

"Oh, I see. Well, in a small place like Nairobi, we all love the gossip."

"Yeah? How many other people have called Dan Dawes for inside information on this case?"

"I didn't ask him. And he didn't say."

"Sorry, but I'm afraid you're tipping our hand."

"Didn't realize we're playing poker."

"I'm waiting to hear the official charges against my father. Was the man he slugged a policeman or not? I'd appreciate knowing that as soon as possible."

"Is this all you're thinking, young Fletcher?" Even in the dim light shed by the hanging lanterns of the lodge's patio, Carr's face was without shadows.

"What do you mean?"

"I don't know. I don't know what I mean."

Surprising warmth flooded through Fletch's body. "Well. I don't know my father." He shook his head. "It would have been natural for him to meet us at the airport." He shook his head again. "I don't know. I may be mistaken."

Carr tipped his head back and finished his beer. "You're thinking something, at any rate. That's a relief."

"My, my," said Carr. "What have we here? A crippled Sheila . . . ?"

"... being held up by Juma!" Fletch yelled.

"What happened?" Barbara leaned forward and looked out Fletch's window.

Flying low over the camp, everything was visible. Sheila was hobbling down from the tents to meet them. A home-made crutch was under her right arm. His arm around her waist, Juma supported her from the left side. Sheila's right leg was in a long cast. They were both looking up at the airplane, laughing. Behind them hurried Raffles with a pitcher of lemonade and glasses on a tray. Sheila tripped on a tuft of grass. She and Juma nearly collapsed on the ground, laughing.

Carr landed the plane wheels perfectly on the slightly uphill track. "The old dear's splintered her drumstick."

Fletch banged the cockpit door open and held it up.

"Poor Sheila," said Barbara.

Fletch said quietly, "And no Walter Fletcher."

Raffles was first to the airplane.

Sheila and Juma were rollicking down the slope, holding on to each other, laughing like two roisterers in the wee hours.

Fletch got out of the plane, then Barbara. They jumped off the wing.

Carr emerged from the cockpit just as Sheila and Juma arrived.

"All's right here," Sheila called out. "All's right with you?"

Standing on the airplane's wing, arms akimbo, Carr said, "Clearly, all's not right here!"

"But it is!" Sheila waved her crutch. "Juma's a hero! At least, to me!"

"How did you crack your kicker?" Carr demanded.

"The bloody corkscrew tipped over on me! There I was, alone in the jungle, as they say, leg broken, full weight of the corkscrew on me, no more able to move than Buckingham Palace, while three snakes were exploring closer to me, thinking nasty thoughts, I'm sure, while also hearing hyenas laughing at a few ripe ones not far off, and out pops Juma from the flora like a Masai *moran*, spear in hand, to stigmatize the snakes, notify the hyenas the show was over, make me as comfortable as possible, run for the Jeep and men to get the bloody corkscrew off me with high alacrity—generally, to save my sanity and my life, in that order!"

" 'Spear in hand'?" Fletch muttered.

"Darling Juma!" Hand around his shoulder, Sheila grabbed him to her and planted a kiss on his ear.

Juma was laughing merrily.

From his elevation on the airplane wing, Carr was studying Sheila's cast. "Simple or compound?"

"Compound," Sheila said proudly.

"Juma set it for you?"

Holding up her encased leg, Sheila said, "Juma did a first-class job!"

"Good for Juma!" Carr said. "We all thank you, sir."

As they were drinking lemonade, Sheila chatted, "When Juma discovered me in the bush, he moved with such speed, brain, and brawn, I was put to right in no time at all!"

Carr shook his head. "Can't leave you alone for a minute."

"Oh, rot," said Sheila. "Next you'll tell me I spoiled your plans to go dancing tonight!"

++++++++++++++++

"I don't know, though, Peter." Over coffee after lunch under the stretched canvas, Sheila looked around at the less than luxurious campsite, walls of jungle three sides, the derelict-looking Jeep, the sluggish river, the corkscrew lying on its side on the riverbank. "Perhaps it's time to pack it in."

Carr picked a cracker crumb out of his lap and put it on the table. "Been thinking the same thing, old dear. Enough gets to be enough."

Still looking around, Sheila said, "Enough is enough."

Carr, Barbara, and Fletch had flown from the Masai Mara early that morning. They had left the two *hôtelières* in Nairobi and refueled.

Awaiting them at the camp had been a mother with a baby whose back had been burned, whom Carr tended as well as he could, and an old man being blinded by cataracts Carr had to send away.

Lunch at the campsite was late, bigger than usual, slower. Sheila's broken leg had prevented her starting the day's digging, and thus it never did get started. They even had sherry before lunch while Sheila and Juma regaled them again, laughing, about Sheila's pain, terror, near death in the jungle; Juma's appearing from the jungle like a *moran*, slaying the snakes with his spear, dispatching the hyenas, reappearing driving the Jeep, engineering the corkscrew off Sheila quickly and painlessly, then setting her compound fracture and creating a beautiful, smooth cast for it.

"I'll be damned if I sell airplane number two over this project," Carr said. "I already sold one airplane to finance this."

"The one your father used to fly," Sheila said to Fletch. "The one your father now has."

"Did he finish paying for it?" Barbara asked.

"Oh, yes," Carr said. "He had that profitable year flying the Uganda border, while the rest of us were refusing to do so."

"And the house in Karen," Sheila said. "We sold the house in Karen."

Juma came and sat at the table with them.

"Hello, hero," Fletch said.

Juma grinned. "Now it's a bigger story than almost any other."

"It wasn't all that much of a house," said Carr.

"No. Not that much of a house. But it was ours."

Juma was looking quite fondly at Sheila. "Sorry you lost your house."

"With two airplanes flying," Carr said, "in a few years we should be able to afford another house. With only one plane flying, I'd expect to be an apartment dweller from now until my dotage."

A man Fletch recognized came out of the jungle toward them. He walked rapidly with a homemade crutch, heeling-and-toeing across the rough ground.

Sheila said, "You do like your peace and quiet."

"Yes." Carr looked around the camp and smiled. "I do."

"Still," Sheila said. "Enough, as you say . . ."

"Also the matter of the lost income. I'm not making money while I'm mucking about down here . . ."

The man on the crutch approached the table. The front of one foot was bandaged. One toe was in a splint. Two other toes Carr had removed with a garden shears a few days before.

In the man's hand were his two toes still wrapped in the gauze.

"A few more days," Carr said. "We'll give it to the end of the month. If we don't find anything encouraging by then, I guess it's back to Nairobi to find an apartment."

Carr looked up at the man on the crutch. *"Habari leo?"*

Leaning toward Carr, the man spoke softly in a tribal language. He held out the bloody gauze with the toes in it.

Juma grinned. He put his head down, near Fletch, and said, "The man wants to know where his toes are." Speaking in Swahili, Carr pointed to the gauze in the man's hand. "Carr says, 'There are your toes.'" Grin widening, Juma said, "'No, no,' the man says, 'I mean where are the spirits of my toes?' Carr asks him what he means. The man says, 'My toes still pain me, but not the toes in my hand, the toes which are no longer on my feet.'"

"Oh, I see," said Fletch. "That happens. Nerves still signal pain to the brain from a severed appendage."

"Now the man wants Carr to cut off the spirit of his toes, so the pain will stop."

Fletch said, "That makes great sense."

Carr's face was looking as if he had just been told he had buried someone who wasn't dead. Clearly, he did not know how to answer the man.

There was a long silence while Carr looked at the man, the toes in the man's hand, the man's bandaged foot, to Sheila, and back to the man.

Juma said, "Witch doctor."

"Yes, yes," said Carr. "Witch doctor. Only a witch doctor can remove spirits . . ."

Carr launched into a long, gentle instruction to the man as to how he must now go to a witch doctor to have the spirits of his toes removed.

"Listen," Juma said to Fletch. "In three days someone is coming by in a truck. He is going to Shimoni. I would like to take you and Barbara with me to Shimoni in the truck. It is on the coast. We can camp there, and swim, catch fish . . ."

"Sounds like fun."

"Do you want to go?"

"Very much."

"And Barbara will want to come?"

"I think so. I'll ask her."

"It won't be such hot work as here."

"Of course, we'd like to help out Carr and Sheila, for as long as possible."

"We'll only go for a day or two."

"Sounds good."

Apparently satisfied, the man on the crutch was heeling-and-toeing it back along the jungle path.

Carr sighed. He looked at Sheila. "I don't know, old dear. Maybe we won't last the month, what with one thing and another . . ."

"How do you know this truck is coming?" Fletch asked.

"It is coming."

"Can you hear it?"

"No."

Before dawn, Barbara, Juma, and Fletch went out to the jungle track west of Carr's camp and waited. They stood silently in the dew almost an hour, hearing the jungle noises turn from nocturnal to diurnal. They had one knapsack among them, which Fletch kept on his back. After a while, Barbara sat down on the dry track. Fletch lowered the knapsack onto the grass. Only after Fletch sat down did Juma.

After the sun was well up, they moved into the shade. Fletch left the knapsack in the middle of the track.

"Thirsty," Barbara said.

Juma disappeared into the jungle. He returned with two grapefruit, which they shared.

"It will come," Juma said.

"You sure you have the right day?"

No vehicle came along the track.

"Yes."

"It's almost noon," Fletch said. "We could have walked to the coast."

"Yes," Juma allowed. "We could walk to Shimoni."

Juma, Fletch, and Barbara had put in two more long days of clearing brush, digging holes, looking for Carr's lost Roman city. Muscle-weary, tired of being slick with sweat, tired of being thirsty, even Fletch had begun to believe, to wish that there was an ancient Roman city underfoot, that some evidence of a different time, a different people, a different civilization would surface. To himself, as he worked, he marveled more and more at Sheila and Carr selling their house, selling an airplane, a part of Carr's business, and devoting eighteen months rooting about in the bush on just hope.

They had started out that morning clean and cool and fed. Watching the birds and the monkeys sporting about near and across the jungle track, they were again glistening with sweat, even in the shade. They were developing a hunger and thirst grapefruit slices did not address.

Fletch said, "I feel guilty just sitting here. I feel we ought to be back helping Sheila and Carr. They said they're going to give up their search soon."

"The truck will come," Juma said.

Fletch said, "Juma. You seem to have become fond of Sheila."

"Yes." Juma's eyes danced in his head. "Nice lady. Good-spirited."

Barbara asked, "Did you actually talk to this friend of yours with the truck?"

"He's not a friend. Not an enemy, either, I don't think." Fletch sighed. "Are we friends?"

Juma smiled. "We'll see."

"Did you talk to whoever this is who is supposed to be coming by in a truck?" Barbara asked.

"No."

"Then how do you know he's coming?"

"He is coming."

"Do you know the driver at all?" Fletch asked.

Juma said, "I don't know. Probably."

" 'Probably'?"

"Then what are we doing here?" Barbara asked.

"Waiting for the truck," Juma said. "There is nothing to decide about."

About one-thirty, a diesel truck carrying bags of cashews ground its gears slowly up the track. Juma asked the driver if they could ride to Shimoni with him.

Of course they were welcome.

Lying on the bags of cashews on the back of the truck, they jounced along to the coast. The truck generated a little breeze, and the cashews smelled good.

Fletch never did know if that was the truck for which they had waited all morning. It was a truck. Eventually, it had come along the track. It did pick them up. It did transport them to Shimoni.

Fletch wondered how to ask Juma if it was the *right* truck.

After wondering a long time, Fletch found himself asking himself the question, *What does it matter?*

36

"What do you think, Juma?" From their table at the roofed, wall-less restaurant on the crown of Wasini Island, Fletch looked across the ocean at mainland Africa. "Is it possible there is a lost Roman city in East Africa, or are our friends just wasting their time and money?"

Juma shrugged. "How can you decide, until you know?"

Barbara said, "Carr said some documentary evidence exists in London. The appearance and military traditions of the Masai are a kind of evidence, I suppose." She smiled. "And then there's what the witch of Thika said . . ."

"She was right about one thing," Fletch said. "I sure am carrying a box of rocks." Under the table, Fletch stretched out his legs.

Juma studied Fletch's face.

Barbara fingered crab meat into her mouth. "I sure would like to help out Sheila and Carr."

"I don't know." Fletch shook his head. "There are a lot of little things, impressions, things I've heard, rattling around inside my head. I haven't quite sorted them out, focused on them yet."

"Are they helpful?" Barbara asked. "What sort of things?"

"I don't know," Fletch answered. "I won't know until I sort them out."

In midday, Juma was eating steamed crab with them. This was a special picnic, in a special place, Juma had arranged for them.

The afternoon before, the cashew-bearing truck had stopped for them to climb down onto the road outside Kisite/Mpunguti National Park. They walked the fifteen kilometers into the park, past the ruins of the district commissioner's house. Fletch carried the knapsack. They had to pay a few *shillingi* to enter the park.

Originally just a fishing camp, still there was little evidence of tourists there. Tents were sparse, well hidden, virtually invisible. The few visitors were so acclimated to the jungle, the beach, the sea, they did not jar the landscape, seascape. The few officials were casual, unobtrusive, helpful. And the commercial fishermen were still curious about, kind to, these visitors to their world.

Immediately upon arrival, Barbara, Juma, Fletch jumped into the Indian Ocean. It being almost as warm as they were, it welcomed them easily, held them a long time.

Later in the afternoon, they stood upon the lip of the cave, Shimoni, the hole-in-the-ground, and looked down. Fletch and Barbara did not know what they were seeing. To them, Shimoni was a hard-packed mud descent into darkness. Something, not a sound, not a smell, something palpable emanated from the cave.

"Do you wish to enter?" Juma asked.

Fletch glanced at Barbara. "Why not?"

"Going down is slippery." Juma looked at the knapsack on Fletch's back.

Fletch put the pack on the ground.

"There are bats." Juma looked at Barbara's hair.

"It's a cave," Fletch said.

"Is it a big cave?" Barbara asked.

"It goes along underground about twelve miles," Juma said.

"What am I feeling?" Fletch asked.

Juma nodded.

He led the way down the slippery slope.

They stood in an enormous underground room, partly lit by the light from the entrance. Barbara remarked on the stalactites, then giggled at the hollow sound of her voice.

Fletch noticed that all the rock, every square centimeter of floor, all along the walls two meters high, had been worn smooth. Even in imperfect light, much of the stone looked polished.

"What was this place used for?" Fletch said.

A bat flew overhead.

"A warehouse," Juma said simply. "For human beings. A human warehouse. People who had been sold as slaves were jammed in here, to await the ships that took them away."

Only the slow drip of water somewhere in the cave punctuated the long, stunned silence.

When Barbara's face turned back toward them, toward the light, her cheeks glistened with tears.

"How afraid they must have been," she said.

Juma said, "For hundreds of years."

"The terror," Barbara said. "The utter despair."

Juma said, "The smell, the sweat, the shit of hundreds, maybe thousands of bodies. The crying that must have come from this cave, day and night, year after year."

The entrance to the cave was wide, but not so wide it could not be sealed by a few men with swords and guns, clubs and whips. The rear of the cave was total darkness. That damp, reeking, weeping darkness extending twelve miles underground, no way out from under the heaviness of the earth, however frantic, however intelligent, however energetic the effort, to light, to air, to food, back to their own realities, existences, their own lives, loves, expectations . . .

There was only one way out of that cave: docile, enslaved.

Juma asked, "Did your ancestors buy slaves, do you think?"

"No," Fletch answered.

"I'm pretty sure not," said Barbara.

Juma ran his bare foot over the smoothness of the floor stone. "You see, that is how we must think of things."

"What do you mean?" Fletch asked.

"I'm pretty sure my ancestors sold slaves. Do you see? Which is worse—to buy people or to sell them?"

+++++++++++++++

They bought a couple of handsome fish at the ice/trading house just after the fishing boats came in, and cooked them on the beach as the sun dropped into the jungle.

Just before full dark one of the casual officials found them. He brought them to a small tent among the palm trees just off the exposed beach, not far from the dock. There was scarcely room for the official, Fletch, Barbara, and Juma to crawl into the tent, but they all did.

Later, standing outside the tent, Fletch asked Juma, "Where will you be?"

The official had wandered off.

Juma said, "I'll be here."

Deciding everything like that, all the time . . . is very hard. Do you mean difficult? . . . or harsh? . . . Does he mean have a nice time? . . . Or we had a nice time? . . . You said we'd be picked up by a truck which would take us to Shimoni, and, after six and a half hours, we were . . . but was it the truck you were expecting . . . ? . . . What is worse— to buy people or to sell them? . . . I'll be here . . .

In fact, after being in the tent together awhile, Barbara and Fletch were too hot to stay there. Their skin was sticky from the salt water, abrasive with sand, wet with sweat.

They crawled out of their tent in the dark. Hand in hand, naked in what moonlight there was, they ambled down the beach. Without changing pace, they walked into the ocean, ducked, broke handclasp, and swam about, playing quietly, going away from each other, and coming back to each other, again and again.

It was a wonderfully important time in that Barbara and Fletch were having a honeymoon beyond any expectation.

Later, on their way back to their tent, they were widely circumnavigating a tall, broad boulder at the edge of the beach. They had been quiet for some time.

As they walked, the moon came to be behind the boulder, slightly above it.

Barbara gasped. She jerked Fletch's hand.

They stopped still.

"Is that a statue?" Barbara whispered.

Standing on the boulder in profile in the moonlight, absolutely still, stood a slim, male figure, feet together, arms at sides, head held high, perfectly erect, in every way.

"It wasn't there before."

"Fletch. I think it's Juma!"

"It is Juma."

Juma's erect penis was a straight rod extending at a perfect ninety-degree angle from the straight, slim rod of his figure. The stillness of Juma's silhouette on the boulder in the moonlight was stunning.

"What's he doing there?" Barbara whispered.

"Just standing."

"He's so beautiful!"

"Yes. He is."

They couldn't help staring at Juma's silhouette a short while.

Finally, silently, Barbara and Fletch returned to their tent.

Again, just before dawn, they crawled out of their tent, to go to the ocean, to swim, to awake fully, to play. The birds had awakened them. The heat, the heavy air under their low-slung mosquito net kept them awake.

In the morning, returning to the tent, hand in hand, they were walking around a bush when they nearly tripped over a tableau of human bodies.

Juma, naked, was asleep on the ground. Two girls, naked except for their necklaces, bracelets, anklets, hair beads, were asleep with him. Juma's head was on the stomach of one girl. One of his legs was sprawled sideways, not heavily, across the hips of the other. Each of the three faces seemed concentrating on the contentment of sleep.

Juma's penis was rising before him.

"The arithmetic of Africa," Barbara whispered. "I'll never figure it out."

A fly was walking up the cheek of one of the girls, toward her eye. Her hand, across Juma's chest, did not rise to brush it off.

Fletch had the strong instinct to brush the fly off the girl's face.

Instead, he pulled Barbara away, silently, by the hand.

Barbara said, "Just like the lion we saw, his body sprawled comfortably over two lionesses."

++++++++++++++

Not much later, Juma found them at the *ducca* where Barbara and Fletch had bought bottles of Coca-Cola and a box of biscuits for breakfast.

Juma had organized the day for them.

Two Italian couples were all that were to sail on the dhow for that day's excursion. The dhow could take eight passengers comfortably.

The Italians and the dhow's crew had assured Juma that he and Barbara and Fletch were most welcome to join them.

Sailing away from the mainland in the dhow, Fletch asked Barbara, "Do you feel grungy?"

Barbara said, "I feel like Carr's Jeep."

Two husbands and one wife of the Italian couples were medical doctors; the second wife said she was the *madonna* of three children. The Italians spoke little or no English; Juma, Barbara, and Fletch had no Italian: they all came to be jolly together with gestures and *patois*.

At first, Barbara and Fletch were shy of the Italians. Sunburned, bug-bitten, their skin also scraped and cut from clearing jungle trails and digging holes, their hair washed only in salt water and conditioned with sand, dressed in cutoff and now ripped-to-shreds nylon ski pants, already they were seeing the healthy, wealthy Italian tourists as being from a different world altogether. They boarded the dhow in well-cut sunsuits, stripped to even better cut swimsuits. Their bodies were strong but pampered. The skin of each of them was unblemished from either sun or bugs. Each recently had had the attention of a good hairdresser. As the dhow approached the reef they all were to swim, the Italians pulled out of nylon sacks equipment which looked fabulous: masks and snorkels, tight-fitting rubber boots, rubber flippers, two underwater cameras. One man even strapped a sheathed knife to his ankle.

Barbara said, "Already I'm suffering culture clash."

"That's okay," Fletch consoled. "Back at Carr's camp, we have some wonderful skiing equipment."

"Shall I try to tell them?" Barbara asked.

"I think not."

Instantly, Juma was open to the Italians. He asked from them and learned the Italian for sails and ship and wheel and islands, water, fish. One doctor proudly showed Juma how the underwater cameras worked.

Fletch had the great tempation to ask Juma, *Where did the two girls go? Where did they come from?* but he didn't.

The dhow's crew of two were wonderful, full of good cheer and humor for everybody, in English, Italian, Swahili, and one other language they kept to themselves. As a joke, they kept offering to the well-equipped Italians the cheap, worn-out, torn goggles and snorkels they had for rent aboard the dhow. They pretended to be insulted when the Italians, laughing, insisted they preferred their own equipment.

The reefs along the Tanzania coast have been blasted and picked dead by entrepreneurs collecting fish and coral souvenirs for "tourist goats." The reefs just north and south of Mombasa are dying rapidly. So the reefs of Kisite are forcibly protected.

The dhow anchored just outside Mako Kokwe Reef.

The non-Kenyans swam for hours back and forth along the reef. Except for the two men with cameras they just goggled the sculptured coral magnified in the sunlight by the water. They were mesmerized by the lacy coral fans waving in the slight, shifting currents, their shadows moving from side to side on the coral or sand floor.

Swimming slowly in the warm water, not even disturbing the surface of the ocean much, Fletch toured the small schools of fish, many more brightly colored than any birds. Best he liked to look at and follow the bright yellow surgeons with the black lines drawn up from their mouths in an apparent, *Nice time* grin. Always, when he first saw these fish, Fletch inhaled too much, too quickly, to laugh, and would flood his mouth and nose with water. He would have to pull his head up above water to laugh happily at the appearance of the fish, at himself, to recover.

Barbara banged Fletch on the shoulder with her hand.

Treading water, she said, "Juma went back to the dhow."

Fletch looked at the dhow. He guessed he saw Juma's head amidship. The crewmen were in the stern.

"When?"

"Some time ago."

"Is he all right?"

"I was with him at first. He doesn't seem at all comfortable in the water. He kept thrashing about and coughing. At first, I thought he was kidding, then I thought he was drowning."

"He can swim?"

"He works too hard at it. He swims like he feels he's being pulled down more than we are."

"He's just catching his breath."

"He went back almost right away."

"He's all right."

"Maybe we ought to go back, too."

"Yeah. In a minute. In a while."

Sailing along then, in early afternoon, the dhow attracted dolphins which swam along with them for a long while, escorting them, appearing to race the dhow, torpedo it from the sides. Definitely they were relating to the dhow and the people on it, making noises back at them, and all the people on the dhow were relating to them, like friends unseen for too long.

After crossing intersecting currents among the islands, enjoying a short, rough ride in the dhow, the crewmen anchored off Wasini Island. The dinghy took the passengers into shallow water.

From shallow water, the passengers walked over ow-ow up to Ras Mondi.

"Hey." Barbara clutched Fletch's hand as they walked carefully over the ow-ow. "We're having a nice time."

"Things are beginning to come together," Fletch said.

Only the party from the dhow was at the restaurant.

Because of the language barrier, the Italians sat at one table; Juma, Barbara, and Fletch at another.

After the sail and the swim they were thirsty for fresh water and only a little beer. Their hunger made them compete playfully for the first food they saw, sesame-ball appetizers. They thought the enormous steamed crabs were a big enough lunch, all there was, and ate them slowly, savoring them. When plates piled high with *changa* and rice cooked in coconut sauce were set before them, they all rolled their eyes, and then cheered.

"Sheila and Carr will be right disappointed if they don't find anything," Barbara said. "Can't we think of something that might help out? At least to console them?"

"All over Africa, people are looking for their pasts," Juma said. "Digging up bones, and pots, and spear tips. You'd think Africa is nothing but a museum."

Fletch asked, "How come there are fish, perch, from the Nile River in Lake Turkana? The two bodies of water are hundreds of miles away from each other. Nothing, no river, flows from one to the other."

Barbara said, "They must have been joined at one time."

"Why are people so interested in their pasts now?" Juma asked. "Why do people come to Africa from all over the world to search for their ancestors, first man, first bone, first fossil?"

" 'Mild curiosity,' " Barbara said.

"What difference does it make?" Juma asked. "The way to the future is the present, not the past."

"It doesn't make a difference?" Fletch asked. "It doesn't make a difference to you that an East Indian elephant was found buried at Koobi Fora?"

"No," Juma said. "What difference does it make?"

Barbara said, "It suggests that at one time Africa and India might have been joined together. Doesn't that mean anything to you, Juma?"

"Sure," Juma answered. "You want me to say East Indians belong here, in Africa."

Fletch asked the air, "Why did I come to Africa to meet my father?"

" 'Mild curiosity,' " Barbara repeated.

"Why did you come, Fletch? You are who you are. What does your father have to do with you? You don't even know him."

"Cultural flow." Fletch spoke to his plate. "Moral flow."

Barbara said, "What are you talking about?"

"I don't know."

"When people look into the past, " Juma said, "they only expect to find good, good things. Supposing they find bad, bad things?"

Fletch asked, "Am I going to find bad, bad things, Juma? You know my father. I don't."

"I think maybe people are better off going into their futures without worrying about, carrying bad, bad things that might be in their pasts."

"I think you're trying to warn me," Fletch said.

"There are people here," Juma said, "people my age, who insist on living the way their ancestors did thousands of years ago. Like that *moran* you saw near Carr's camp. That's too much of a burden, on all of us. You can't run a computer with a spear."

"Spears come in handy, too," Fletch said. "There are still snakes. You used a spear to rescue Sheila."

"And a Jeep," Juma said.

"Here's something about the future," Fletch said. "Carr told me that someday the Rift Valley is going to rip open at the top, and the Red Sea is going to come flooding down. There will be a sea where there is now a valley."

Barbara said, "They know the future, in this case, from studying the past."

"Things change," Fletch said.

"Yes," Juma said. "Things change. Nomads know that. Constantly we move away from our pasts, because things change."

Fletch said, "Things change . . ."

"You've stopped eating," Barbara said to him.

Juma asked Barbara, "You like leather fish?"

"Leather fish?" Barbara asked. "I'm eating leather fish?"

"*Changa*," Juma said. "Leather fish."

"Oh, my God." Barbara looked at the little left on her plate. "I'm eating something called leather fish."

Fletch said, "I'm thinking about the Mississippi River."

"There are no leather fish in the Mississippi River," Barbara said. "Catfish. I don't like to eat catfish, either."

Fletch said, "It is also said the Mississippi River is going to change course."

"Right," said Barbara. "Then New Orleans will really be blowin' the blues."

"Rivers change course, sometimes," Juma said.

Fletch shook his head, as if to clear it. "I'm beginning to have an idea. All these things I've heard, rattling around in my head—"

Juma said, "Carr and Sheila are digging along a river that exists now." He laughed.

Fletch said, "Thousands of years ago . . ."

Barbara put down her fork. ". . . the river might have been somewhere else."

"So Carr's *theory* might be right . . ."

". . . but the river might have moved," Juma chuckled.

"Oo, wow," said Barbara.

"Of course the river might have moved," Juma laughed. "Why didn't you ask me?"

"Nice time," Fletch said. "Let's go back to Carr's camp."

"Can't move," Juma said. "Ate too much."

"Absolutely!" Swooping the airplane through the sky in joy, Carr dipped the wings.

"No doubt about it!" Barbara was in the seat behind Carr.

Juma was beside her, trying to look out all the airplane's windows at once. "Looks good!"

"Carr," Fletch said, "I need to be set gently on the ground."

"You mean, it's true?" Her encased leg stuck out into the airplane's aisle, Sheila had to shout from the rearmost seat. "There was another river?"

"*Naam, Momma!*" Juma shouted. "*Indio!*"

Everyone was shouting over the noise of the engine.

"Damn!" Carr swooped the plane lower for another horizontal look, this time from the west. "All the times I've flown over this area, and I never noticed. Damn me!"

"Soon," Fletch said.

"That line of trees, all the way to the ocean, is distinctly different," Barbara said.

"The whole line is indented," Juma said. "You see? A different growth. Deeper in the ground. Greener, too."

"Absolutely." Looking through his side window, Carr was flying just above treetop level. "From this level, you can see the gap."

"Carr . . ." Fletch moaned.

Juma, Barbara, and Fletch stayed at Kisite/Mpunguti one more night. It was late when they returned to the mainland. Juma said one did not start a long trek into the jungle an hour before sundown.

"Only superstition, of course"—Juma smiled—"but the ancient belief is that people might, just might, get lost in the jungle after dark, might just get hurt, might not be able to protect themselves so well from snakes, zebras, warthogs, cheetahs, and lions." He lowered his head as if ashamed. "Just an ancient African superstition."

"Then I guess I'm superstitious," Barbara said.

"Anyway," Juma said. "After eating so much we are too stupid and lazy-sick to do anything but trip around in circles until we fall down. We deserve to be snacked up by hyenas."

At dawn they stood by the main road. An iced fish truck going to Mombasa took them part of the way. After walking an hour, an old Kenyan *née* English farm couple picked them up in a Land-Rover they said they had brought to Kenya thirty-six years before. It jounced along well. Juma knew when to start walking again through the bush.

They walked most of the way back to camp.

Early afternoon they found Carr and Sheila with a team of workmen setting up the corkscrew for another dig down-river. Sheila stumped around on her crutch, being as helpful as she could be. Clearly, though, from the expressions on their faces, the way they moved, Sheila's frustration had grown, Carr's patience had thinned.

That afternoon, in the steamy jungle, Sheila and Carr would have listened to any idea.

Sitting in the shade of a baobab, Barbara, Juma, and Fletch explained the possibility they had thought of, that sometime during the last two or three thousand years the river had changed course. They should look for signs of another river in the area, one that no longer existed, one that might have existed in times of the Roman Empire, upon the banks of which the Romans might have built their city . . .

Hearing the excited talk, the workmen worked themselves closer, then stopped, to listen.

After listening, Carr studied Sheila's face. "What do you think, old dear?"

Sheila shrugged. "It's possible, I suppose."

"Do you suppose we could spot such a thing from the air?" Carr asked.

"Yes," Barbara said firmly.

"Maybe," said Fletch.

Wearily, Carr stood up. "I suppose it's worth taking the plane up for a spin. I'm beginning to feel like an earthworm anyway."

Making a chair by clasping their hands and wrists together, Fletch and Juma speeded the laughing Sheila up the riverbank, through the camp, to the airplane.

Having the idea the dry riverbed might be there, they spotted it almost immediately. A wandering, snakelike trail departed from the river five kilometers north of the camp to the right, the west, and wandered discernibly through the jungle on a longer course to the sea.

Following it, Carr pointed through the windshield and shouted to everyone. "You see? At some time in history, the river fell to lower ground, took a shorter course to the sea."

"Water takes the course of least resistance," Sheila piped up from the back, "unlike some reasonably intelligent people I know."

Carr was taking them all for a spin in the airplane—literally. He followed the dry riverbed to the sea. He flew low, at treetop level along it, to the east of it. Swooping up and down, crossing back and forth, he was proving to himself and everyone that the dry riverbed was distinguishable from all heights, all angles.

Fletch was sick.

Quite suddenly, he found himself fighting not to vomit. Below them, the landscape was moving much too fast, tilting, coming and going. His vision blurred. His head pounded as if stuffed with rusty pistons in a rapidly accelerating engine. The back of his neck tightened to pain. As well as he could, he sucked huge amounts of air into his lungs.

A very different sort of sweat was on his face, the sort that made his skin feel distant to himself, and cold.

"Carr," he groaned. "I think you'd better put me on the ground soon."

"Look!" They were high in the air again. Barbara was pointing forward, so that Carr could see. "Look at that little hill."

"Look at that!" Carr banged the heel of his right hand against the control panel. "Right where I figured! A lovely big mound on a bend at the west side of the river, how far from the sea?"

"Maybe ten kilometers," Juma said.

"That much, you think?" Carr spun the plane around and down, down again to the large mound next to the dry riverbed. He flew over it and around it several times. "If there's not a city under that hillock," Carr said, "I'll eat a zebra raw!"

Barbara said, "You just might."

Carr was really showing what he could do with an airplane that afternoon.

When the airplane fell, Fletch's stomach remained in the air. When the airplane rolled, Fletch felt his stomach was going to be splattered out through his sides. When the plane climbed, his stomach met itself just coming down with a lurch.

His head wanted to burrow into the soft earth below.

Getting into the airplane and taking off, Fletch had felt well enough.

Shortly after takeoff, he felt a stab of pain in his eyes. Afternoon sunlight reflecting from the windshield of another airplane, far away, seemed to cut right through his brain.

Breathing hard through lips that felt like sausages, Fletch knew he could not contain vomit much longer.

He grabbed Carr's forearm. "Carr!" he shouted. "I'm sick! Really sick! Please put me down on the ground as soon as you can!"

"Tender tummy?" Carr examined Fletch's face. "You've never complained of it before." He rolled the plane into a left turn. "Hold on!"

Only to Fletch did the rest of the flight seem interminable.

He heard Carr say, "Hello. Look what the hyena dragged in."

Fletch opened his eyes. The airplane was approaching the landing track leading uphill to the camp.

At the top of the track was parked a yellow airplane with green swooshes. The cockpit hatch was open.

A man in khaki shorts and shirt stood beside the plane, watching them land.

++++++++++++++

Fletch not only had the cockpit door open, but his seat belt off before Carr's plane touched the ground.

While the plane was still taxiing, Fletch crawled out onto the wing. As soon as the plane slowed, he rolled off the wing onto the ground, which, thankfully, did not move.

Kneeling, Fletch vomited onto the ground.

The plane came to a complete stop fifteen meters up the track. Everyone was *hello*ing and offering to help Sheila disembark.

Trying to keep his back to everyone, while trying not to kneel in his own vomit, trying to find new places to vomit, Fletch walked sideways on his bare knees across the track.

Behind him, near the airplane, there was much excited talk. He heard the name Walter Fletcher. The names Barbara, Juma. Happy, happy talk about the new hope of their finding the lost Roman city. Comments about Sheila's broken leg and Juma's heroism. Something about the Thorn Tree Café.

The voices were approaching Fletch.

He scraped his knees a little further along the dirt.

"And this," he heard Carr say, standing over him, behind him, "is Irwin Maurice Fletcher. Bit under the weather at the moment, as you can see. 'Fraid I did one too many loop-de-loops for him."

Surveying the long trails of vomit and knee scrapes he had left across the track, Fletch wiped his nose and his lips and his chin with his hands.

Then, using his hands to push himself up from the ground, he stood up. His knees felt as if they had never worked, never bent, never clicked straight. They wobbled. His lower back felt like a rusty crane.

He took a deep breath.

He turned around.

Carr looking solid, arms akimbo, Sheila on her crutch, one foot off the ground, Juma smiling uncertainly, eyes dancing, Barbara dressed like a drugged Sunset Strip tart, hair dirty, sweat and dirt sworling on her skin, stood with a stranger among them, all looking at Fletch.

The stranger said, "He's a pretty poor-lookin' specimen, isn't he?"

Everything below Fletch's waist went numb.

He raised his face, for air. His eyes closed against a spinning sky.

When his knees hit the ground, the back of his neck snapped forward. His right shoulder was shot with pain as he landed badly on his arm, twisting it.

The hard rain did not begin until late the next afternoon.

Fletch had a raging fever.

Looking up, Fletch saw Carr's face looming above him, looking larger than normal. Above Carr's head was the peak of the tent. Fletch did not know how he came to be on the narrow cot in a tent. His legs ached. His head ached. He was cold. Sweating cold. His mouth tasted filthy. His right shoulder pained. He did not know the source of the pain in his shoulder.

"How do you feel?" Carr asked.

Fletch thought it all through again. "Wonderful."

"That's good."

"May I have a blanket?"

"Sure." Carr stuck a thermometer in Fletch's mouth.

Barbara's round-eyed face was over the end of the cot. Arms folded across his chest, Juma stood near the tent flap.

Raffles came in and covered Fletch's body with a brown blanket.

Carr removed the thermometer and studied it. "At least now we know it wasn't my superb flying that laid you low."

"I'm hot."

"I'll say you are."

Carr fed him a glass of cold soup and two pills.

"Pity," said Carr. "We're planning fettucini with a nice anchovy sauce for dinner."

Consciousness coming and going, Fletch marked time through the night. He heard pots and lids banging in the cooking tent and then talk and laughter from the eating tent. Carr came to see him again, shook him awake, said something Fletch couldn't remember long enough to answer, gave him two more pills, more cold soup. At some point, he saw Barbara's face in the low light of the kerosene lamp. Then silence, long, long silence. Carr came again during the night. He helped Fletch sit up, take more soup, more pills. For a while, Fletch remained awake under the mosquito netting, conscious now of the raucous jungle noises. Hot, he tossed the blanket off. Cold, he pulled it back up to his chin.

Carr was there again in the morning. He read the thermometer in the daylight near the tent flap. "May you live as old as this reads," he muttered. More soup. More pills.

"How do you feel?"

"Wonderful."

"That's good."

There were more happy noises from the cooking tent, eating tent. Someone kept whistling the first four bars of that popular Italian song. Over and over. Maybe it was a bird.

Juma stood beside Fletch. He said nothing.

After a long while, Carr was in the tent with Barbara and Sheila.

Carr said, "You awake?"

"Wonderful."

"We're going to trek through the jungle to that mound we saw yesterday. Do you remember?"

"Sure. Mound."

"See if we can dig up anything. Pick-and-shovel brigade. You'll be all right?"

"Sure."

"Sheila's staying here. Can't drag her through the jungle anyway. She'll keep putting fluids into you, and pills."

"Okay."

"We'll be back."

"Right. Good luck."

"You'll be better when we get back," Carr said.

"Absolutely."

Carr's big bulk moved away from the cot.

Barbara asked, "You want me to stay?"

Fletch wanted her not to have asked. "No."

"I can stay."

"No. It's an exciting day."

"You'll be all right?"

"Go find the lost Roman city. You don't want to miss that."

"I really believe it is there."

"Hope it is."

"If you rather I stay . . ."

"No. Go with them. Go."

". . . okay."

Barbara left the tent sideways.

Sheila's voice seemed stronger. "You want anything now?"

"No. I'm fine."

Sheila left.

Distantly, Fletch heard the Jeep start. Voices called to each other. The Jeep's engine accelerated. There was a shout, a squeak of brakes. The Jeep started off again.

Raffles came in and washed down Fletch's body with cold, wet rags. It felt wonderful. Raffles even turned Fletch on each side, to wash his back thoroughly.

"Raphael?"

"Yes?"

"Will you bring every blanket in the camp, please, and pile them on top of me?"

"Well. Okay."

During the morning, Raffles and Winston entered the tent, not saying anything. They picked up the cot with Fletch in it and carried him outside. It was a surprisingly dark, gloomy day. They set him evenly on the ground under a tree.

Winston put a camp chair next to the cot.

"Rain?" Fletch asked.

"No," Winston said. "Many times it looks like rain here, but there is no rain."

Sometimes when Fletch awoke, Sheila was sitting in the chair, sometimes not. Sometimes she was leaning forward, working a wet rag over his face and chest. She gave him soup and a lighter, cold herb tea and the pills while either Raffles or Winston held his head up.

"Are they back yet?" Fletch asked.

Sheila said, "No."

"You should be with them."

"I'm glad to be with you."

"What time is it?"

"Never mind."

Going and coming. The day got darker rather than brighter. The air was heavy.

It was a long day.

Again, Fletch awoke in the tent. He didn't remember being carried back.

Carr was standing over him, smiling.

Fletch hadn't heard the Jeep.

"How do you feel?" Fletch asked.

"Wonderful!" Carr held his hand out. Fletch did not reach for it. Carr held something up for him to see.

"What is it?"

"Pottery shard. You can see a piece of what is distinctly a Roman soldier walking with a spear and a shield."

"Fabulous!"

Carr held up his other hand. Something glinted in the low kerosene light.

"And, in case you have any doubts about what we have found, look! A coin!"

"No!"

"Yes!" Carr laughed. "Showing the head of Caesar Augustus. Or so we think. Wasn't he the pretty one?"

"They were all pretty, as boys."

"Definitely Caesar Someone."

"My God!"

"And I think we may have found the top of an ancient wall. Pretty sure of it."

"Carr, that's wonderful!"

"I'll say. Sheila's outside doing the Masai jump, which ain't easy on a crutch."

"What's that?" Fletch heard something like clods of dirt being thrown against the tent.

"Rain."

"It's going to rain?"

"Probably not."

"Carr. Congratulations. Good news. Sorry I wasn't there."

Barbara came in behind Carr, to see how Fletch was.

"Fine."

Carr said, "I'll be back later, to take your temperature."

Later, the sound of the rain was wild. Fletch heard none of the cooking, dining noises. The tent sides were billowing from the gusts of rain.

Fletch watched the water seeping in from under the tent sides. A few rivulets first, turning into brave streams, as well as a general dampness growing in from the sides, all sides; soon there were good-sized puddles inside the tent.

Carr was soaking when he came in.

He turned up the kerosene light on the box to read the thermometer. Frowning, he said, "You're pretty sick, Irwin."

"Sick of Irwin."

"You should be better."

"I agree."

"You can only keep up these high temperatures so long, you know."

"How long?"

Hands on hips, Carr watched how the rain beat down on the tent. "Can't fly you out to the hospital in Nairobi in this weather. Can't take off." He looked sideways and down at Fletch. "You've got to get better."

"My legs, Carr."

"What about 'em?"

"They feel awful."

"Like what?"

"All broken up."

Carr pinched a toe on each foot. "Can you feel that?"

"Yes."

"Can you feel that?"

"Yes."

"It's just the fever."

"They feel all broken up."

More soup, more pills.

Fletch awoke while Raffles was washing him down again.

Fletch wanted all the blankets back on him.

The three blankets were soaked through. They weighed like lead.

Leaving, Raffles had to fight with the tent flap to secure it down against the wind and the rain.

Later, when Fletch awoke, Juma was standing over him silently. In the low light from the kerosene lamp, Juma's hair and skin glistened with rainwater.

Fletch said, "Not a nice time."

"You know what?"

"What?"

"You've got to put down that box of rocks."

The muscles in Fletch's lower stomach heaved.

Juma helped Fletch throw up, on the ground, on the side of the cot away from the tent flap.

Then Juma was there, wet again, with a broom, pushing the vomit and the mud around it out of the tent. He held the bottom of the tent up with one hand while he swept the vomit out under it.

Alone, Fletch listened to the rain. It was interesting watching the vomit seep back in, under the tent wall.

When his stomach felt better, he rolled onto his back.

"Oh!" Fletch jumped awake.

There was a terrible smell in his nostrils.

Huge, red-veined eyes were staring into his from only a few centimeters away. His ears were filled with a weird, high crooning. There was pressure, warmth, against his forehead, and against his heart, and his penis and scrotum were warm. It was not the warmth of the jungle heat or the warmth of the fever. It was a different, drier, more real, more human warmth.

Looking down as much as he could from the staring eyes, Fletch saw the nose, the cheeks of an old face. Orange streaks were painted on the face.

The breath of the crooning old man was horrible in Fletch's nose, mouth.

The old man's forehead was pressed against Fletch's. The old man's left hand was pressed against the skin of Fletch's heart. The old man's right hand was cupped in Fletch's crotch, over his penis and scrotum.

Breathing into Fletch's face, the old man was crooning up and down the scales.

Fletch said, "Jesus Christ."

When he awoke, the old man was gone. Had he dreamt it? The stink was still in his nostrils. The three wet-heavy blankets were smoothed over him again, from toe to chin.

He felt no better from the event, the reality, the dream. Except for the lingering smell, he felt no worse.

Box of rocks.

Then Carr, bare-chested, wet, was shaking more pills out of a bottle.

Fletch did not remember taking them.

The sound of the rain, pelting the ground outside, hammering against the tent, went on and went on and went on.

✦✦✦✦✦✦✦✦✦✦✦✦✦✦

Suddenly, Fletch's eyes were wide open. The low light from the kerosene lamp had not changed. The box on which the lamp stood, as well as the wet towel on the box, was suddenly clearer in Fletch's eyes. The seams of the tent over his head were more distinct.

The air seemed cleaner in his nostrils. The ache in his head was gone, until he moved his head too quickly.

His arms were happy to move, lightly, as they were ordered.

He was free, free of the fever.

Through the sound of the rain he heard men talking. Two men. Their voices came and went under the sound of the rain.

No one was in the tent with him.

Realizing how heavy, wet the blankets were, he pushed them off him, to the bottom of the cot. Lying down again, he raised his legs, brought his knees to his chest, straightened them, let them down.

Free.

A decision had been made.

Bare feet in the mud, Fletch sat on the edge of the cot and tried to think about the decision. He listened to the rain. He felt cool, normal. There was nothing to think about.

The decision had been made.

This was right. This was normalcy. This was health. This was being alive. If he wanted to be open to life, health, normalcy, *rightness*, he also had to be open to the decision, commit himself to it, act on it, because the decision was based upon decisions made by everybody, everywhere, a long, long time ago, *in the beginning*, and those decisions, once made, determined how everything worked, life, health, defined normalcy, and if one, anyone, did not act basically within those deductions, or acted against them, or decided something else, then *legs*, which hold us up, support us, permit basic movement, progress, *shatter*, and shortly we are sitting in the dust, all of us, corrupt and cracked-headed, corrupting, awaiting the jackals.

Tired rising from the cot, dizzy at first, Fletch stood a moment sucking in the jungle air, heavy with rain. He could smell the jungle, the rotting roots and the slashed green leaves. He could hear the noises of the animals as they moved around in their world, acting within decisions, what was normal, what was health, what was life for them.

Making choices is the ultimate freedom in a world in which decisions have been made to permit such freedom. Failure to see that sometimes no choice can be made, that there is no personal decision, is the ultimate folly, the absolute destruction of self and all.

Fletch took the wet towel and tucked it around his waist.

Pushing aside the tent flap, he looked outside. There were signs of dawn in the sky. The rain was a nearly solid, straight-down torrent, hitting so hard it made the ground look almost jumping.

From which direction was the sound of two men talking coming? Two men, talking loudly over the sound of the rain, in English. Laughing. Listening through the opened tent flap, just inside his tent, Fletch could not make out what they were saying.

A tent across the way, newly put up, showed dim light around the edges of its flap.

Unsteadily, the rain beating on him, feeling good, feeling weary, feeling fresh, feeling slightly dizzy, Fletch splashed and slithered across the campside mud barefooted.

Do I have to do this? Am I sure I have nothing to decide? The decision has been made. We exist within context. That is our first, our only, our last decision. Making choices is the ultimate freedom. There is no freedom without basic decisions having been made. Self-discipline is the greatest exercise of freedom.

He pulled aside the tent flap and looked in.

Inside, Peter Carr and Walter Fletcher sat in canvas, wood-framed camp chairs. Each had a glass in hand. On the box beside the kerosene lamp was a nearly empty bottle of whiskey.

They stopped talking. They stared at Fletch.

The lines in their faces moved up from around their mouths to around their eyes.

Fletch said to Walter Fletcher: "Thanks for coming to the airport to meet us."

The two men sitting in the tent staring up at Fletch through the dim light of the kerosene lamp said nothing.

"Do you speak Portuguese?" Fletch asked the man with the thinning, combed hair, pencil moustache.

"What do you mean?" asked Walter Fletcher.

Fletch stood just inside the open tent flap. Behind him, rain poured with a steady roar.

"I saw you," Fletch said. "At the airport. In the men's room."

"Oh, my God!" Carr sat forward in his camp chair. "Say it isn't so."

On the box beside Carr, next to the kerosene lamp, next to the whiskey bottle, were the pottery shard and the Roman coin.

Walter Fletcher stared full-eyed at Fletch. He put his whiskey glass on the box. He resettled himself in his chair.

Ankles crossed, boot heels in the mud, hands folded in his lap, for a long moment Walter Fletcher studied Fletch's face.

Slack-jawed, Carr was staring at Walter Fletcher.

For only a second, Walter Fletcher glanced at Carr.

Then he looked at Fletch, for another long moment.

"Well." Abruptly, Walter Fletcher stood up. His boots were flat in the mud. He patted down the pockets of his safari jacket. Using both hands, he smoothed back his hair from his temples.

Chin up, not looking into Fletch's face, he brushed by Fletch. He walked out of the tent into the storm.

"Where is he going?" Fletch asked.

"Nowhere he can go." Carr remained hunched over in his camp chair. "What a box of rocks. All this time, you've been thinking the murderer at the airport could have been Walter Fletcher."

Fletch shrugged. "The murderer was a local who came to meet someone at the airport . . . whom he did not meet."

"Don't you think you'd better sit down?"

"Jesus, Carr!"

"What now?"

Fletch had heard an airplane engine ignite. Carr had not.

They both heard the roar of the engine as gasoline was pushed into it.

Carr jumped up.

Together, Fletch and Carr stood outside the tent looking through the heavy rain in the dawn across the campsite at the yellow airplane with green swooshes. The cockpit lights went off. The wing and tail lights were on.

The airplane was turning around over the rough, wet ground. Wings rocking, it skittered around Carr's plane and jounced onto the landing track.

"A plane that light can't take off in this heavy rain," Fletch shouted. "Can it?"

The glass in Carr's hand had a centimeter of rainwater in it already.

Carr said, "I wouldn't try it."

The airplane almost made it. It splashed and swayed down the track. Its engine roared through the sound of the rain. Throwing water behind it, it lifted off the track. It rose against the tree line. For a moment it looked as if it were above the treetops.

The left wing dipped. The plane fell.

The plane's left wing cracked against the top of a tree. The treetop shook. The tip of the wing fell into the woods. As if pivoting, engine roaring, the plane swung left around the top of the tree.

Then only the undercarriage of the tail of the airplane was visible against the sky.

From the woods was not a crash, but a thud.

Instantly, flame was visible through the undergrowth.

Carr thrust his glass into Fletch's hand.

"I'll go. You're in no condition—"

Carr ran splashing through the rain.

"The flames. Carr—"

Fletch threw the glass aside. He ran, tripping over the wet ground, slipping in the mud.

Fletch hadn't gotten far when he fell, facedown in the mud. He tried to get up, quickly. His head felt cement. Pain shot from his right shoulder. Weak from his days of fever, his arms and legs flailed the mud uselessly.

He lay stomach on the ground a moment, his right cheek, ear in the mud, just breathing.

He watched air bubbles in the mud break open.

Rain-soaked, muddy from head to foot, a cut bleeding on his forearm, Carr entered Fletch's tent.

Carr shook his head, *No.*

Fletch was sitting on the edge of his cot. Mud ran down his face, the front of his body, his chest, his stomach, into the sodden towel around his waist; down his legs into the mud at his feet.

How many words did my father speak to me? He's a pretty poor-lookin' specimen, isn't he? *No. These were not words spoken to me, but about me. He said,* What do you mean? *He said,* Well. *Five words. My father spoke five words to me. In my life. In his life. In our lives.*

I had no decision to make.

The basic decision ordering how people behave, for survival, the social contract, was made a long, long time ago.

"Carr, he was trying to get away. Wasn't he?"

"Who knows?" Carr said. "Who cares?"

"My mother said he was apt to evade moments of emotional intensity . . ."

"How do you feel?"

". . . like being hung from the neck."

In the dim kerosene light Carr watched Fletch from across the tent.

"He finally died in an air crash. In a storm. Not in Montana, but in Africa. *Presumed dead.* The courts made a presumption, which was almost right."

"All this noise apparently hasn't awakened anybody."

"The sound of the rain . . ."

"Yes. The sound of the rain."

"How did he get to be here? I never heard."

"You've been pretty sick."

"Were the charges against him dropped?"

"All that was a joke already. Another funny story. The *askari* had no official standing. He was just an unlicensed guard from a jewelry store across the street. So Walter was released from custody after paying a fine, damages to the Thorn Tree Café, the *askari*'s hospital expenses, plus a few *shillingi* to make up for the weight the *askari* gained in hospital."

"I came halfway around the world to put my father out into a storm; to see him killed in an air crash. Poetry."

"Irwin . . ."

"Yes, Carr."

"I know you can't be feeling like a calisthenics director on a spring morning . . ."

"How I Spent My Honeymoon."

"This is Tuesday. A plane leaves for London tonight. I think you and Barbara should be on it."

"Yes?"

"As soon as the weather clears, I'll fly you up to Nairobi, book your seats."

"Okay." Fletch fingered mud from his eyes. "Anything

you say. You've been a real friend, Carr. Thank you."

"Enough of that. I thank you. If it weren't for the intelligence of you and Barbara and Juma, we never would have found the world's latest ruin."

"Having found it will make a big name for you, Peter Carr."

"Yes. I want to go to Nairobi today and report the find. Show the evidence. Turn the whole dig over to the scientific wallahs. After discovering the place, I don't want to be accused of messing it up."

"Right. Discover, but do not meddle. Be committed, but not involved."

"Also, of course, I have to report the death of Walter Fletcher to the authorities, get them down here."

"Yes."

"In the meantime, we still have the problem of the police accusing someone innocent of murder."

Fletch looked up at Carr's solidity. "We're not going to report Walter Fletcher was the murderer?"

"Not unless we have to. Why should we? Why totally wreck the name Walter Fletcher? It's a small world."

"You're thinking of me."

"If it looks like they're going to hang the wrong bag, you'll come forward?"

"Of course."

"Then there'd be a reason for coming forward."

"Maybe it will be an unsolved crime. But Dan Dawes—"

"This morning you might write out an eyewitness account, beginning in the men's room at the airport, including the events of this morning. Maybe I'll show it to Dan Dawes."

"Okay."

"If the authorities come even close to indicting someone else for the murder, I'll hand your account in officially. See if they want to bring you back to testify."

"Sounds like the best thing to do. I guess."

"I'll get you some paper and a pen. A spot of tea might go well about now, too."

"Carr? Why are Barbara and I leaving so soon? Why are we leaving tonight?" Across the tent, still standing, ignoring the cut on his arm, Carr looked at Fletch without expression. "I'm thinking about a funeral. My father . . . The excitement of the discovery . . ."

"The air crash will be investigated," Carr said. "The authorities will be here. University people will come to see the ruins. The press. They'll all be here by tonight."

"So what?"

Carr took a step closer to Fletch. Even in that dawn's light, Carr's eyes were clear, blue. Quietly, he said, "Don't you suspect your passports are phonies?"

At Los Angeles airport, looking into her passport, Barbara had said, *Where did this picture of me come from?* Fletch had never seen his passport picture before either.

"Well. I know we didn't apply for them ourselves."

Carr nodded.

✦✦✦✦✦✦✦✦✦✦✦✦✦✦

"I've heard all the news." Wet, bedraggled, Barbara stood inside Fletch's tent.

Propped up on the cot, the kerosene lamp pulled close to him, Fletch was writing out his account of the murder of Louis Ramon and the death of Walter Fletcher in an air crash during a storm.

Before starting, he had showered most of the mud off him in the rain.

My father did not die in childbirth.

Barbara said, "I don't know how I feel about it."

"How you feel?"

"No." She continued to stand a meter away from him.

Sweat, humidity: Fletch was having difficulty keeping the paper dry to write.

"We need to get packed," Fletch said. "We're starting home tonight."

"Once we came here to camp, we never really unpacked. Just underwear."

"I guess we don't need to pack the torn sweaters and cutoff ski pants."

"I'll hang them from the trees. Maybe the monkeys will wear 'em. Suits them."

"Still. We must repack."

"It's not as if I'm overburdened with souvenirs."

"You have some memories. For the long ride."

"I never even sent my mother a postcard."

"You can send her one from home. Where's Carr?"

"In his tent. He's writing something, too."

"His version of events."

"He says he thinks it will clear up enough for us to take off at noon."

Fletch looked out through the tent flap Barbara had left askew. "Can't take off in this rain."

Barbara said: "So I heard."

"Your father was a murderer." Barbara was buckling herself into her airplane seat aboard the midnight flight to London from Nairobi. "Won't your mother love that? Think of all the books she's written looking for the murderer."

Fletch was already buckled into his seat. He sighed.

He said nothing.

He had a long way to go with the other passengers aboard.

He had a long way to go with Barbara.

After they were airborne and the No Smoking sign went off and the stewardesses demonstrated to the passengers what to do if the airplane ditched and the Fasten Seat Belt light went off, the voice over the public address system said, "Will passenger Fletcher please identify himself. Mr. I. M. Fletcher?"

Building a nest for herself in her seat, clearly Barbara did not hear the request.

Fletch took a deep breath and closed his eyes. *Don't you suspect your passports are phonies?* More trouble could wait.

The rain had not lightened enough for them to take off from the camp until afternoon. Packing the airplane, Carr made lame jokes about the skis. No one looked down the runway track to where an airplane had crashed that morning, burned itself up; where there was still a corpse.

There was a good-bye scene of mixed emotion. The workmen, including Winston and Raffles, said good-bye individually. Sheila had hugs and kisses for Fletch, Barbara, and Juma. They were all sad to be parting, sad to be standing near a terrible death, yet each quite glad that something sought at great expense had been found, that a historic discovery had been made, and that each had been part of it.

Nor did Fletch look down for the burn hole in the woods as they took off.

He did not put on his new white sneakers, courtesy of the Norfolk Hotel, until they landed at Wilson Airport.

Juma and Carr helped them with their luggage to the International Airport. Juma stood with them while Carr took their return ticket to the airline counter.

The few people who were in the airport at that hour looked curiously at the skis.

Fletch said to Juma: "Nice time."

Juma's head tilted. "Sorry."

"You have seats on tonight's flight." Their tickets and boarding passes were in Carr's hand when he returned. "You have to take your luggage through Customs yourself. Do you have any Kenyan money? You have to turn it in."

Both Barbara and Fletch dug out the few Kenyan shillings they had and handed them to Juma. Laughing, they both said: "No."

Money in hand, Juma bent over laughing.

Carr said, "I'm afraid you'll have to wait a long time. The plane doesn't leave until midnight."

"We'll be all right," Fletch said. "I need to sit down."

"You'll feel all right on the flight?"

"Sure. I need the rest."

"Well." Carr looked around the nearly empty terminal. "There are things I must go do."

Fletch said, "I understand."

"One happy, one sad."

"You'll arrange for a funeral?" Barbara said.

Carr hesitated. "Oh, yes."

Fletch said, "Carr . . . Peter Carr, we thank you—"

"No, no." Turning away, his face reddened, Carr waved down Fletch's speech. "Don't embarrass us."

Barbara said, "Thank you, Peter Carr."

Fletch hugged Juma. "I'll see you on television, kid."

"See you on the funnies pages."

While Barbara hugged Juma, Fletch hugged Carr. Then there was a general shaking of hands all 'round.

" 'Bye," Carr said. "Fletch."

Fletch said to Juma: "Friends?"

"Why not?" Juma asked. "Nice time."

Fletch tilted his head.

The wait at the terminal seemed interminable. Barbara read magazines. Fletch thought over the account of the murder of Louis Ramon and the death of Walter Fletcher he had written and handed Carr.

Slowly it dawned on him that he had another story to write. A story much better than the stories of avalanches, mud slides, major earthquakes, airplane crashes, train wrecks, mass murders, airport bombings Frank Jaffe had requested. He had the story to write of Sheila and Peter Carr, the story of their historic discovery of the ruins of an ancient Roman city on the east coast of Africa.

After thinking about it, Fletch decided he would not mention to Barbara just yet that he would get a story for the newspaper out of their honeymoon.

Barbara nudged him. "That's you."

"What's me?"

"They just paged you. 'Would passenger I. M. Fletcher please identify himself?' she just said."

"Oh."

Fletch raised his hand. There were people milling about in the aisles.

"Maybe we get a free bottle of champagne," Barbara said. "That would nice."

"You're always hoping."

"Mr. Fletcher?"

"Yes."

The stewardess handed him a letter.

"Mail delivery in midair?" he asked.

"Someone sent it aboard requesting it be delivered to you after takeoff. Would you like a drink?"

"No, thanks." Opening the envelope, Fletch said to Barbara, "It's from Carr."

"Oh. No champagne."

The letter read:

Dear Irwin:

The plan was that after meeting and greeting you and your bride, the man Walter Fletcher and I were going to take you aside and quietly explain ourselves.

Instead, the man Fletcher understood he was to meet you at International Airport and got himself into his own trouble, as you and I both know.

As you now must realize, the Kenyan government takes their official documents very seriously indeed. With the man Fletcher in jail, I suddenly saw him, and you and Barbara, as loose cannons careening around the deck. Forgive me, but I think you can understand I did not want my particular ship to sink, not at this point in my life.

The facts are these. I was in Kenya at the time English colonists had the choice of either going back to

England or of turning their English passports in for Kenyan citizenship. I had flown planes in Chile, Australia, Colombia, then here. Even I had come to the point where I wanted to be a part of somewhere, of Kenya. While in Colombia, I had faked out heavy smuggler types, causing several to be shot, and they had proven slow to forgive. Occasionally, therefore, odd people would appear, looking for me, and I'd have to go hide in the bush until they went away. This was inconvenient. Always when they left they would leave the message that they would keep looking until they found me.

At the same time, Peter Carr had heavy debts he couldn't pay, both in England and in France. I never inquired too deeply into the nature of his difficulties, but I believe they were severe.

Peter was English; I, American.

With only a little doctoring, during those days of official confusion, we switched passports, my American for his British, which I turned in for Kenyan. People who subsequently came looking for Walter Fletcher found Carr, and did not shoot him; people who came looking for Peter Carr found me, and left me similarly intact.

Thus we lived peacefully for years.

I realized I was taking a risk in inviting you and your bride here, but one, I thought, we could survive.

I was only half right.

I don't deserve to be reported well to your mother, I suppose. We are grown-up people now. For each other, we can never be children again.

We were children when we married.

There was a storm the night in Montana I took off to fly home, just having had the news of your birth, but I never saw the storm. I landed at a small, closed airport just before dark. See in your mind's eye, if you can, a boy, a teenager, sitting in the cockpit of his airplane at the end of a runway of a small, closed Montana *airfield, a blizzard raging a few miles ahead of him, a very young husband who had just been told he was a very, very young father, shivering, feeling, thinking. More than my feet were cold. It was not Josie, my wife, I was rejecting. It was not you, Irwin Maurice, my son, I was rejecting (despite your moniker). I was rejecting myself that night, the idea of myself, as husband and father. That night I knew, as an absolute certainty, that I would be a terrible father, a terrible husband, a total disappointment, that I would cause more pain than we all could stand. There was no doubt in that boy's mind, sitting in the dark, shivering in the cockpit, that you would be better off without me. I could have flown into the side of a mountain that night. I didn't. For us all, I took the next option: disappear, get out of your lives, go have my own accidents without you as victims. Two days later, in British Columbia, I read of my probable demise. I left it at that.*

Even so, I know I have caused you both much pain. Through the international brotherhood of flying buddies, I have had occasional reports, photographs of each of you. You've done okay without me; better I think, than you would have done with me. The history of my achieving my present maturity would gray the hair and crack the spine of even the most casual but consistent observer. I've barely survived it myself.

If you cannot report well of me to your mother, someday you might let her know I read her books as love letters I don't deserve.

To you, my son, I offer a simple, sustaining thought: one mellows.

I appreciate your having enough mild curiosity to come see me.

What astounded Fletch was that the letter written to him
was signed *Fletch*.